THE MAMMOTH ADVENTURE

PHILIPPA GREGORY

Illustrations by

Chris Chatterton

HarperCollins *Children's Books*

First published in Great Britain by
HarperCollins *Children's Books* in 2021
HarperCollins *Children's Books* is a division of HarperCollins*Publishers* Ltd
1 London Bridge Street
London SE1 9GF

www.harpercollins.co.uk

HarperCollins*Publishers*
1st Floor, Watermarque Building, Ringsend Road
Dublin 4, Ireland

1

ISBN 978–0–00–840329–4

Philippa Gregory and Chris Chatterton assert the moral right to be identified as the author and illustrator of the work respectively.
A CIP catalogue record for this title is available from the British Library.

Typeset in Georgia 13/24pt by Sorrel Packham
Printed and bound in the UK using 100% renewable electricity at CPI Group (UK) Ltd

MIX
Paper from
responsible sources
FSC™ C007454

For Freddie and Sebastian

Contents

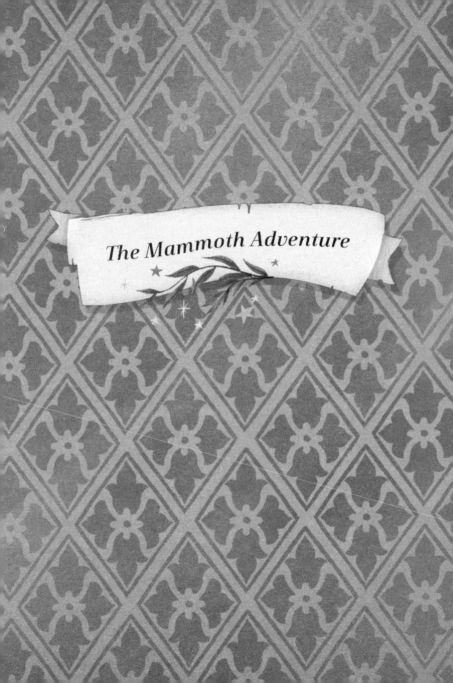

The Mammoth Adventure

CHAPTER ONE

*In which two guests outstay
their welcome (it is very rare
that anyone wishes a Sea
Serpent would stay longer)*

'What *is* going on outside?' the king
demanded crossly.

The queen listened. There was a noise like
thunder: *PAD-PAD-PAD-PAD-pad-pad-pad-
pad* followed by silence. Then it began again.
PAD-PAD-PAD-PAD. Then they heard a great
swooshing noise, like a wave breaking on a
shore, and a cross voice said, 'You moved! I
saw you!'

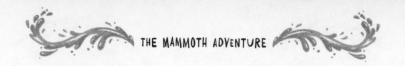

Through the turret window, they could hear a giggle. 'Did not.'

Next came a sound like an ebbing wave, and then a sudden thunder of footsteps, and the same voice cried out in triumph: 'Home! I'se home! I win! I'se home!'

'What in Fairytale Land *are* they doing?' the king demanded.

'That's six – four to me,' it said. 'Go back to the start. Round eleven coming up.'

The king joined the queen at the window to watch their two inconvenient guests.

'They're playing a game like Grandmother's Footsteps,' she said wearily. 'The Sea Serpent is under the drawbridge like a troll, and the

Mammoth has to get across like a Billy Goat Gruff. The Sea Serpent pops up and if it sees the Mammoth move, he has to go back to the beginning again. If he freezes before the Sea Serpent comes up, he stays quite still, waits till the Sea Serpent goes underwater again and then races to the end of the drawbridge.'

'But that noise, like a hundred cannons firing rounds of shot all at the same time! Is that the Mammoth tiptoeing?' said the king.

'Yes,' said his wife shortly.

'It's like thunder,' the king remarked.

'Undoubtedly,' the queen agreed.

'*Undootedly!* And they have been playing this game for how long?'

'All summer,' the queen said through gritted teeth. 'Every single day.'

'Will the drawbridge stand the weight?' He peered out again as there was another great rumble of noise and the castle rocked. 'Is he dancing now?'

'That's his celebration,' she said. 'A special dance on his hind legs. He does it every time he gets to the end of the drawbridge without the Sea Serpent catching him.'

'That drawbridge is going to collapse into the moat if they carry on like this,' the king said crossly.

'It's the guards I feel sorry for,' the queen agreed. 'Every few minutes, the Mammoth comes charging over the drawbridge and then they all have to salute and shout, "Halt! Who goes there?" and the Mammoth just giggles.'

'And who is to blame for all this chaos in my royal palace?' the king demanded, puffing himself up so that his uniform tightened over his chest and his medals jangled. 'Name the culprit!'

The queen shrugged. They were both thinking of the same person.

'Name her!' The king made it quite clear who he was blaming.

'You know as well as I do,' the queen said. 'It's Florizella of course! She thought it was only fair to keep the Mammoth in the Seven Kingdoms after he got magicked here by accident. And we all agreed that the Sea Serpent should get an allowance in picnics if it would give up eating princesses. We saw no problem about it living in the moat – except it *is* a bit embarrassing for us when we have visitors. But nobody dreamed they would become such good friends. Nobody imagined this game. Nobody could have thought that they would play it all day, every single day.'

'Well, somebody *should* have thought of it,' the king said grandly. 'And I know who!' He stalked to the royal office door, opened it and shouted down the spiral stone staircase, 'Florizella!'

He waited for a moment. In the sunny silence, he could hear the birds singing, the hens sleepily clucking in the orchard and the bees droning in the rose garden. It was all very peaceful and quiet, then – *PAD-PAD-PAD-PAD-pad-pad-pad-pad*, and the Sea Serpent whooshed up and the Mammoth froze.

'Sssaw you,' the Sea Serpent hissed, and the Mammoth ran heavily back to the start of the drawbridge and waited for his friend to sink under the bridge so he could begin creeping across again.

'Hi, Daddy King, hi, Mummy Queen!' Florizella ran up the spiral stairs and came into the room. She was wearing her jodhpurs and hard hat. Her brother Courier came in behind her, wearing a full riding habit with a skirt that looped elegantly over his arm. In their own ways, they both looked great. But neither mother nor father was pleased to see them. Florizella looked from one cross face to another. 'Is something wrong?'

'Listen!' her father said crossly. 'Just listen. And you tell me if something's wrong!'

Florizella and Courier stood still and listened
to the thunderous tiptoeing of the Mammoth
and the swish of the Sea Serpent as it reared
up out of the moat and cascaded back down. In

the guard tower, the sentries flinched, as the wave of green water from the moat splashed over their perfectly shined boots and perfectly pressed trousers, and braced themselves for the galloping arrival of the Mammoth.

'But what seems to be the problem?' Courier asked, looking at his father's face with interest. 'The Mammoth and the Sea Serpent are playing nicely. And yet you seem disturbed, my dear father.'

'*What seems to be the problem?*' the king harrumphed. 'Seems? The problem? What? To be? *To be?*'

'My very words!' Courier exclaimed, pleased that his father agreed with him so exactly. 'In a different order, but the sense is there, and that's the main thing, after all. What seems to be the problem, Mummy Queen? You also appear to be upset.'

'It's the noise,' she said simply. 'The noise of the Mammoth running and stopping, and the Sea Serpent rearing up and splashing back into the moat, over and over. All day, every day. The Mammoth is far too heavy for the drawbridge, and the guards are getting wet when the Sea Serpent dives. And they're very tired of shouting, "Halt! Who goes there?" a hundred times a day.'

'Oh! These guys! These guys!' Courier said fondly. 'I thought you'd be pleased they were outside playing in the sunshine, and not stuck inside on their screens.'

'They don't have screens,' the queen reminded him. 'Nobody has screens here. This is Fairytale Land, remember? They've not been invented.'

'No, of course! Would you like me to invent them?'

'No.'

'Seems a bit of a pity. What do children do all day without screens to watch?'

'They play,' the queen said. 'They play outdoor games like . . .'

PAD-PAD-PAD-PAD – scuttle-scuttle. 'I'se won! I'se won! I got there!' came a squeaky bellow from outside.

'Like that,' the queen said.

Courier raised his eyebrows with a little smile as if he was thinking that she might prefer their two guests to play all day on video games instead of destroying the castle drawbridge.

'But, Mummy Queen, do think how nasty the Sea Serpent was in the past,' Florizella pointed out. 'This is so much better than it used to be.'

The queen exchanged a glance with Florizella. A Sea Serpent's job was to eat a princess unless her prince arrived first to save her. Those were the old Princess Rules that prevented girls from doing anything interesting, or even defending themselves. The queen had nearly been eaten by the Sea Serpent not just once, but twice. It was only Florizella refusing to obey the Princess Rules, and Courier and Prince Bennett giving up the Prince Permit that meant girls could not be picked on ever again. Not by Sea Serpents, not by anyone.

'This is as bad as being eaten,' the queen said,

flinching at the thunder of the Mammoth's celebration dance as he reached the castle gatehouse once again.

'It can't be,' Courier said reasonably. 'This is disturbance. Not digestion.'

'It is very loud,' Florizella agreed. 'But there are one hundred and thirty-four rooms in the palace. Can't you move the royal office to one of the rooms at the back?'

'So that the Mammoth and the Sea Serpent are free to play on the drawbridge?' The king was outraged. 'Why can't *they* move? And, besides, if anyone comes to visit – Bennett's parents from the Land of Deep Lakes for instance, or the king and queen from the Utter West – how does it look if they can't ride over the drawbridge because there's a huge

Mammoth on it playing silly games? And a Sea Serpent rearing up from the moat underneath and hissing at them? What are they going to think?'

'Oh, if I was them, I would think. . .' Courier began, but Florizella gently leaned on him to make him stop talking. Courier was always very helpful when someone asked a question, but this was one of the many occasions when it was better for a new prince to say nothing. And it was one of the questions that grown-ups – even kings – don't really want answered. It was a question like: 'What do you think you're doing in the fridge?' Or: 'How did you get so muddy?'

'Why are you leaning on me?' Courier asked his sister. 'Don't lean on me! Stand up straight while I explain what the king and queen from the Utter West might think if they found their path blocked by an enormous Mammoth playing Grandmother's Footsteps.'

'I know that you are just dying to explain,' Florizella replied. 'But the question was rhetorical.'

Courier loved a new word, as Florizella very well knew. 'What's a rhetorical question?' he asked eagerly.

'One that doesn't need an answer,' Florizella said. 'Such as: will you ever learn to be quiet when the king is upset about something that we've done?'

'No answer required?' Courier checked.

'None at all,' his sister agreed.

'Rhetorical – like what makes you think you have the right to tell me what to do?'

Florizella gritted her teeth. 'Rhetorical,' she agreed.

'Got it,' Courier said. He turned to his father. 'You don't want an answer to that,' he assured the king. 'What you want is someone to stop the Mammoth and the Sea Serpent blocking the drawbridge, making such a noise and playing in the moat.'

The king looked hopefully at his son. '*Undootedly*,' he said. '*Undootedly.*'

'Luckily for you,' Courier reassured him, 'you've got me.'

CHAPTER TWO

*In which they send for
Bennett - and he comes
surprisingly quickly*

lorizella and Courier were sprawled
on the bank of the moat, dabbling
their feet in the greeny water and talking to
the Mammoth who was stretched out on the
bank beside them. The Sea Serpent's long
sinuous body was floating in the water with its
head resting on the grassy bank, its beautiful
sapphire eyes shining. Florizella was trying to
explain to them that their game was making

the castle shake and nobody could get on with their work.

'It's not as if you DO anything, is it?' the Sea Serpent asked with a sly little smile. 'What *is* it that you do all day? What are we interrupting? I take it you're not declaring war on anyone, or opening anything?'

'My mother, the queen, and my father, the king, are working royals,' Florizella said primly.

'And I'm a working Sea Serpent,' the Sea Serpent pointed out. 'You just mean that I am what I am. But it doesn't mean I actually DO anything. I used to eat princesses – now that was real work. Occasional – but regular. But you won't even let me do that now.'

'Those days are gone,' Courier told it firmly.

'So none of you royals need to learn how to

fight a Sea Serpent,' it pointed out reasonably. 'So, if you're not going to war, or saving princesses, or opening something, I don't see what you actually do. Nobody ever attacks you. What do you need the drawbridge for? Or the moat? We're the only ones that make any use of them.'

'Don't you wike us any more?' the Mammoth asked piteously.

'We do! We do!' said Florizella, putting her arm round his enormous neck and hugging him. 'We love you. We always will.'

The Sea Serpent widened its beautiful blue eyes at her. 'Do you love me too, Florizella?'

'Why?' she asked cautiously.

'I love you ssso much I could eat you,' it hissed with a wicked little smile.

'Those days are gone,' Courier repeated sternly.

'And why do you hiss?' Florizella demanded. 'You sound like Courier when he lost his teeth. Have you lost a tooth?'

'I'm a Sea Serpent,' it told her. 'A serpent is a sort of snake. Courier told me. So I hiss like a snake.'

'A sea serpent is called a serpent but actually it's not a snake,' Florizella corrected it.

'What then?' the Sea Serpent said sulkily.

'I don't know? Something like a newt?'

'I am nothing like a newt!' the Sea Serpent exclaimed indignantly.

'I'll look it up and tell you,' Courier reassured it. Courier loved a fact, or a new word, or an invention. 'You're much more like a snake than a newt.'

'Anyway, the point is that the drawbridge wasn't built for your sort of game,' Florizella told them. 'It's going to break. And the castle shakes when you do your celebration dance, Mammoth.'

'Can't you build a new castle?' the Mammoth asked.

'Not really,' Florizella said. 'But maybe we could find somewhere that would be better for the two of you. Perhaps a lake with a big strong bridge across it so that you could play your game there?'

'And picnics.' The Sea Serpent licked its lips at her. 'Remember that if I don't have picnics I'll go back to eating princesses. I'd ssssuccumb.'

'You can't,' Courier told it firmly. 'I have

given up the Prince Permit, and Florizella has given up the Princess Rules, and you have given up the Sea Serpent Allowance. That was agreed.'

'Yessss,' the Sea Serpent said reluctantly. 'That was agreed *then* – when you invited us to live at the castle. But *this* is a quite different proposal.'

Courier started to look a little anxious. 'Well, shall we at least ride out and see if there is somewhere you would like better than the drawbridge?' he said. 'Somewhere with a bit of variety? And picnics too, of course.'

'I'll send for Bennett to come with us and help us,' said Florizella. 'He can bring a picnic – you'll enjoy that.'

The Sea Serpent widened its deep blue eyes

at her. 'I am sure you hope that I do,' it said with silky menace. 'Sssscertain.'

The Seven Kingdoms did not have a postal service, they had messenger birds. Bennett had five or six parrots living at Florizella's castle, and she had a little flock living at his, so they could talk all the time. Florizella called a small bright red parrot named George out of the aviary and taught him her message.

'*Bennett, come at once. Father cross. Mammoth trouble. Need a brilliant plan. Bring a picnic. Come quick!*'

She looked at the parrot,

who seemed rather confused. 'That's it,' she said. 'That's all. Can you remember it?'

The parrot nodded and then repeated the message two or three times in his squeaky little voice: '*Bennett come at once. We have Mammoth trouble. Father cross. We need a brilliant plan. Bring a picnic. Come quick! That's it.*'

'You don't need to say "that's it", you silly thing,' Florizella said fondly. 'I said it because that was the end of the message. That's it! That's all. Just remember the message.'

Gravely, the little parrot nodded and Florizella lifted him up high into the sky, pointed his beak towards the Land of Deep Lakes and set him free. Spreading his little scarlet wings, George headed off towards

Bennett's castle. Florizella smiled as she watched him go, but then she heard him cry, '*Bend it! Come and dance! Massive trouble. Father cross. Need a brilliant ham. Bring a piglet. Some quick! That's it.*'

'No!' she shouted up at him. 'That's not it! Come back!'

But the parrot could not hear her. He was battling a strong breeze and practising his message. '*Bend it! Come and dance! Massive bubble. Father cross. Need a brilliant ham. Bring a piglet. Some sick! That's it.*'

'No!' Florizella yelled again. But the bright red parrot was just a little orange dot against the blue sky.

'Do you want me to invent the telephone?' Courier appeared at her elbow.

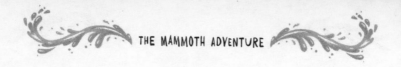

'No!' Florizella said crossly. 'This is Fairytale Land. We don't need phones. We have a brilliant bird messenger system. George is one of our best parrots. Bennett will know exactly what I mean.'

Bennett was paddling in a little coracle on one of the many lakes of his kingdom. A coracle is a round boat that was first made in Flatland by people in the Bronze Age – so it's probably the oldest boat shape ever made. It looks odd to us because it's shaped like a bowl. (Of course a Bronze Age person would look at our rowing boats and say, 'Why so thin? Why so uncomfortably narrow? Where are you going to park your broad Bronze Age bottom? Why,

oh why, row backwards?) Bennett had made his coracle from bendy bits of willow tied together like a bowl, then he had covered it with waterproof cloth, and launched it on to one of the Deep Lakes. He remembered the Prince Permit, so he stayed within his depth. He had been taught:

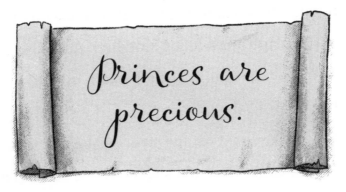

Princes are precious.

And this was just as well because, as George the messenger parrot circled in the sky, it was very clear, even to the parrot who was thinking of nothing but his message, that

Bennett was slowly sinking. The round shape of his coracle made it difficult to steer in a straight line, so Bennett was going in circles. The waterproof cloth wasn't as waterproof as he had thought, and within minutes he was sitting in a puddle. Soon it was a deep puddle. Worse, it was getting deeper and deeper as the coracle sank lower and lower in the water, until only Bennett's head, shoulders and his hands holding the paddle were above the water.

George the parrot, reciting his message over and over to himself, flew down and perched on the paddle.

'Oh! Glad to see you, George! Lucky you're here!' Bennett exclaimed. 'Please fly at once to the lifeboat station and tell them to launch.'

'Got a message,' said George, racking his brains for the exact words.

'Tell it to me later,' Bennett said, feeling the coracle sinking below him, deeper and deeper, and now settling into the mud at the bottom of the lake.

'Important message,' George said, scowling with concentration.

'Yes! Good! Tell me afterwards,' Bennett said impatiently. 'But right now go to the lifeboat station and tell them to rescue me! Tell them Emergency! Please!'

George held tight to the paddle with his little feet, fluttered his rosy wings, put his head on one side and shouted as loud as his squawky little voice could manage. *'Massive bubble! Father lost! Need a brilliant clam. Bring a piglet. Come quick. That's it.'*

'What?' Bennett said. The water was creeping up his neck. Now he was standing on the little bench seat in the coracle, so as to keep his head out of the water. The water was extremely cold, and small fish were nibbling at his shirt. He couldn't be blamed for his irritation. But the way he shouted 'WHAT?' upset George, and even more of the message flew out of his little red head.

'Father lost in massive bubble,' he said. *'Needy boiling clams. Bring a piglet. Come. Thick. Nitwit.'*

'Did you call me a nitwit?' Bennett demanded. He was really angry now. 'Did you call me a thick nitwit?'

There was a sudden screaming noise from the

sky, as if a tornado was bearing down on the lake. Bennett ducked and the parrot sitting on the blade of his paddle cowered from the gale.

'Did someone call a member of the royal family a nitwit?' demanded a booming horrified voice. 'A nitwit? A thick nitwit?' It was a Good Manner Eagle, the most feared of all etiquette coaches, swooping down from the sky in a mighty stoop, and snatching Bennett's paddle with George sitting on one end, and Bennett holding on tight in the middle.

'No!' squawked George. 'Not me! Not me! It was a message from Princess Florizella.'

'Florizella called me a nitwit?' Bennett demanded.

George had a sudden doubt 'Or maybe it was "that's it". Or nitwit.'

'Makes a bit of a difference!' Bennett gasped as, with one huge flap of its mighty wings, the Good Manner Eagle carried them up into the sky. George was clinging to the paddle for dear life with Bennett hanging below it, gripping as hard as he could. The coracle was hooked round his feet, pouring water on to the fields far below.

'We'll see what Her Royal Highness has to say about that,' the Good Manner Eagle ruled.

'No!' Bennett cried. 'It doesn't matter!'

'Nothing matters more than courtesy,' the Good Manner Eagle replied. 'Princes pride themselves on their politeness.'

'Really, I don't!' Bennett gasped. But nothing would stop the Good Manner Eagle. Beating its great silvery wings it flew towards

the palace, with the paddle, George the parrot perched on it, and the dripping coracle with Bennett swaying below.

It only hesitated when it saw Florizella, Sea Serpent, Mammoth and Courier sitting on the bank of the moat, wondering if Bennett would come soon and if he would bring a really good picnic.

The Good Manner Eagle wheeled round and released its incredibly strong talons and the coracle dropped down and hit the moat with a mighty thump and a huge splash. Bennett landed in it amidships, knocking the breath out of him as, with a frightened squawk, George and the paddle came down together and clattered on Bennett's head.

'Gosh,' said Florizella, extremely surprised

as the Good Manner Eagle landed on the grassy bank of the moat beside them. The Sea Serpent – an aquatic creature itself – took a long, interested look at Bennett and the coracle, slid like a snake into the moat and circled him.

'Sssssspeedy arrival,' it hissed. Bennett could not speak – the drop into the moat had winded him.

'Less than ssstable,' the Sea Serpent told him, examining the coracle with an expert eye.

'Obviously,' Bennett gasped.

'I sustain doubts that your little ship will float,' it told him.

'That,' Bennett replied with exaggerated politeness, as his coracle started to fill with

water, 'I think I know.'

'To ssstate the obvious,' the Sea Serpent pointed out, 'you're ssssinking.'

CHAPTER THREE

In which a VUP - a Very Unpleasant Person - arrives

'Oh, get him out!' Florizella shouted, springing to her feet.

'He's been very rude,' the Good Manner Eagle pointed out. 'Him and a very insulting parrot. Unless it was you?'

'That's a royal messenger parrot. One of Bennett's own birds. I don't think it will have been rude to him.'

'Then it must have been you. Did you call

him a thick nitwit?' The Good Manner Eagle turned its stern yellow gaze on her. 'Is that the way to address a prince?'

'No, but . . .'

'Is that the message you sent?'

'No! Of course not!'

'Stating the obvious,' the Sea Serpent repeated from the moat. 'I am supporting him. I am his sssole sssupport. Is it sssink or ssswim?'

It had wrapped its shiny green coils underneath the coracle so that Bennett looked like a baby bird in a round nest on a bough.

'Bring him out!' Florizella begged.

'And the picnic?'

'What picnic?'

The Sea Serpent's beautiful blue eyes, now

gleaming with hunger, glanced towards the little red parrot who was sitting on the paddle blade, preening his wing feathers.

'That is a parrot, not a picnic,' Courier explained.

'Sssame thing?' the Sea Serpent said hopefully.

'Not at all. I say, Bennett, you're very wet.'

'Sssstating the obvious,' the Sea Serpent said again, and brought Bennett, the coracle, the paddle and the parrot to land. Florizella heaved her friend out of the coracle, and the bedraggled prince dragged his unreliable craft on to the bank of the moat.

'If you want a boat, I think I can invent a better one than that,' Courier started. 'What about a hovercraft?

'No,' the other two said at once.

'Bennett, what's going on?' Florizella asked him. 'I just sent a completely simple message asking you to come over. We need your help. We've got trouble with the Mammoth.'

The Mammoth rolled his dark eyes towards Bennett. 'Sowwy,' it said.

'It's not your fault,' Florizella said kindly.

'What message did you send me?' Bennett asked. 'Because the eagle thinks you were rude. George – tell them what you said.'

George puffed out his little scarlet chest, enjoying the attention, and put up his crest. '*Father lost in massive bubble. Speedy boiling clams. Bring a piglet. Lump! Thick! Nitwit!*'

The Good Manner Eagle gave George a long, hard look. 'To whom are you speaking?' it asked.

George's red crest wavered and sagged a bit. 'Just repeating the message.'

'He is not!' Florizella said crossly. 'I never said anything like that! Of course I didn't! It's complete gobbledegook.'

'Wobbwedewook,' said the Mammoth quietly to the Sea Serpent. 'Compwete wobbwede-wook.'

'But what did you actually say?' Bennett asked. 'Since I'm here anyway.'

'Father lost in massive bubble . . .' the Good Manner Eagle prompted her.

'Father cross. Mammoth trouble...' Florizella translated.

'Speedy boiling clams?'

'Need a brilliant plan.'

'Oh,' said Bennett. 'Obvious when you know what it is.'

'Bring a piglet?'

'Bring a picnic!' Courier exclaimed.

'Or you could have just brought a piglet,' the Sea Serpent suggested. 'A little fat juicy one?'

'No!' Florizella said. 'And "Lump! Thick!" was "Come quick!"'

'But nitwit?' challenged the Good Manner Eagle. 'That was the worst of it.'

She thought for a moment. 'It wasn't part of the message at all. I said, "That's it."'

George put his crest up again and nodded triumphantly. Clearly, he thought he had done a great job.

'Better to send a letter,' the Good Manner Eagle advised Florizella. 'Address at the top right-hand side, date and then "Dear Bennett", and what you want to say – something polite about how you hope he is well, and end "Yours sincerely". That's the polite way to send a message. Much better than using a parrot. Especially one with no memory and a ridiculous tendency for muddle.'

'I am so sorry,' Florizella said gravely. 'I didn't mean to inconvenience you.'

'Not at all,' the Good Manner Eagle said grandly, leaping up and soaring into the sky where it circled far above them, as if still keeping an eye out for any instances of impoliteness.

'Wittle bit fwightening,' the Mammoth confided, peeping upwards and huddling a little closer to Florizella. 'Wather stwict.'

'So, what is the trouble?' Bennett asked. 'Now I've come all this way and been dropped and got wet and been thumped on the head by a paddle and insulted by a parrot. And why is your father cross? He's hardly ever cross.'

'He doesn't like the game we play,' the

Sea Serpent told him. 'We're breaking the drawbridge. And he doesn't like us sssspilling the moat. Or frightening the sssentries. They find me sssscary.'

'Well, you can understand that,' Bennett said fairly. 'You're hissing like a snake.'

'Yessss,' the Sea Serpent agreed with quiet pride. 'I just ssstarted.'

'And we bwock the dwawbwidge,' the Mammoth confessed. 'When the king has a visitor, and he doesn't wike that. Wook! Here comes someone now!'

The three royal children turned to look. Rumbling down the road came a coach. The two older ones said at once, 'Oh no!', and Courier, who had not met this visitor before, said, 'What an odd-looking lady. Who is that?'

'That's Countess N'Asty,' Florizella told him. 'The worst witch in Fairytale Land.'

'Her name is Countess N'Asty?' Courier checked.

'Yes,' Bennett said. 'Nobody likes her.'

'Obviously they don't!' Courier said. 'What chance does she have to make friends with a name like that?'

CHAPTER FOUR

In which (at last!) someone actually wants the Sea Serpent to visit

With Courier way out in front and Bennett and Florizella trailing behind, the three royal children made their way along the bank to meet the Countess N'Asty at the drawbridge. The Sea Serpent slid into the moat and swam beside them. The Mammoth stayed well back in the orchard, creeping from tree to tree, believing himself to be completely hidden by the trunks.

The Countess N'Asty had once been a famous beauty. Her hair was stiffly curled in blonde ringlets, her eyes were fierce and dark, and, when she snarled, she showed broken and chipped yellow teeth. Her face was scrunched up now in a hideous scowl and her shoulders were hunched, as if she were ready for a fight.

'Hello!' said Courier pleasantly, not at all

dismayed by the furious glare she turned on him. 'I'm Prince Courier and this is my sister, Princess Florizella, and our friend Prince Bennett.'

'I know,' snapped the Countess N'Asty. 'I've not come here to see you. I've come to see the king and queen.'

'My dear parents,' Courier told her smoothly.

'I am sure they will be delighted to receive you. Shall I show you in? Will you leave your – er – horses out here?'

They were not really horses – they were extremely bad-tempered large black cats that the countess had harnessed to her rackety coach. They snarled at Prince Courier until the Sea Serpent reared up from the moat and rested its long green chin on the drawbridge, looking at them with a hungry smile. Then they sat down and washed their paws of the whole business.

'They can come out and meet me,' the countess said. 'I'm not stopping.'

Courier glanced up at the Good Manner Eagle circling above. 'As you wish,' he said. To Florizella he whispered, 'Why don't the Good

Manner Eagles grab her? She's so rude!'

Florizella shook her head. 'They gave up on her years ago.'

'Most unfair,' Courier said quietly. To the Countess N'Asty he said: 'I'll tell them you're here. I'm sure they'll be delighted. What name shall I say?'

She scowled at him. 'I am the Countess Not-Nasty,' she said.

Bennett giggled and the Good Manner Eagle dropped down to perch on the battlement of the castle above his head. Bennett stopped giggling and tried to look very respectful.

'Of course,' Courier said smoothly. He crossed the drawbridge and went into the palace, as the countess turned to look at Florizella and Bennett. 'In my day,' she said, 'princes and princesses were beautifully dressed and beautifully behaved. All the time.'

With the Good Manner Eagle's narrowed gaze on them, Florizella and Bennett just bowed as if they were sorry for one of them being soaked through and the other a little dusty – which they were not.

'How old are you?' she asked Florizella and, without waiting for the answer, she said, 'Shouldn't you have left home and be unhappily married by now?'

'Unhappily married?' Florizella queried.

'In my day you went to a princess-choosing ball, you got married and you lived unhappily ever after. That was how we did it in Never-Ever-Land. That was my home. It was called

Never-Ever-Land for short. It's real name was "Really hope it's only once upon a time, can't stand it to happen twice, but wish it was Never-Ever-Land.'"

'And don't you live there now?' Bennett asked. 'In Never-Ever-Land?'

Countess N'Asty gave a little growl and the bad-tempered cats glanced at her to see if they were all going to be asked to scratch someone. 'I got thrown out,' she said crossly.

'What for?' Florizella hardly dared to ask.

'Being too nasty,' she admitted. 'I upset everyone. I picked on everyone. I didn't just bully little kids, I was mean to important big people too. So they threw me out and I moved to the Shady Side of the Mountain, where I live in Great Ill-humour and Grumpiness.'

'Oh, that's a shame,' Florizella said. 'I'm so sorry.'

The countess showed no gratitude for the sympathy. 'Great Ill-Humour and Grumpiness is the name of the town,' she said. 'You can keep your sympathy for yourself. I love it there. Everyone is in a bad mood in Great Ill-Humour. The only people who are more miserable than us in Great Ill-Humour are those who live in Grumpiness.'

'How are they in the Slough of Despond?' Bennett asked, making a little joke.

'Stuck,' she replied bluntly.

The Mammoth sidled up behind Florizella and rested his trunk on her shoulder. 'I wike it here,' he whispered. 'We won't go there, will we?'

They were relieved to see Courier crossing the drawbridge, leading the king and queen, with Samson, the wolf who lived in the palace like a pet dog, trotting behind them.

'Good morning, Countess N'Asty,' the queen said. She was wearing her best crown, as she always did when she had an unpleasant visitor. Behind her the king looked stern and dignified.

'This drawbridge is a mess,' the countess said, without even saying hello. She waved a hand at the Mammoth, the Sea Serpent, the soaking-wet prince, the scruffy princess and the little prince with his perfectly curled golden hair. 'And this lot! What on earth d'you think they look like?'

'My daughter, Princess Florizella, her friend Prince Bennett, and my son, Prince

Courier,' the queen said icily. 'And our friends, Mammoth and Sea Serpent.'

'Ridiculous,' the countess growled .

The king said nothing because he did not like the countess and he didn't want to know what she thought, even if he agreed with her. 'Harrumph,' he said.

Courier glanced over at his father. 'Harrumph?' he queried. 'I've only seen it written in books. I've never heard anyone actually say it.'

'Quite,' the king said.

'Anyway, I've got a complaint,' the countess interrupted.

'You always have a complaint,' the queen pointed out.

'I want to come into your kingdom and

collect things. But the royal guard on the border says I can't.'

'It depends what you want to collect,' the king said cautiously. 'You can't collect my guards, for instance.'

'Or any of our people,' added the queen. 'Certainly not the children.'

'Who would want them?' the countess demanded. 'No, I have a show of Rare and Disagreeables. It's a very good show. I'm in it myself.'

'Are you rare?' Courier asked.

'No, but I'm disagreeable,' she said. 'Extremely.'

'You know, that's vewy twue,' the Mammoth whispered, his trunk in Florizella's ear.

'You can collect Rare and Disagreeables if

they want to join the show,' the queen said. 'But you can't take anyone who doesn't want to go.'

'I like the look of that . . .' The countess pointed at the Sea Serpent who was half out of the water, leaning on the drawbridge.

The Sea Serpent opened its mouth in a yawn and lolled out its green tongue. It snapped its jaw shut and smiled at the countess. 'I am rare,' it agreed. 'And I can be dissssagreeable. I am *both* rare and dissssagreeable and – to tell you the truth – I have outssssstayed my welcome here, in this rather ssssoupy moat. Sssso, I will join your show. But I will need an enormous tank. I am not a sssnake.'

'No,' said Courier, bursting with information. 'You're an amphibian.'

The Sea Serpent turned its blue gaze on him 'I am?'

'Amphibians are creatures that breathe air and water.' Courier said, reading from the notebook where he recorded new and interesting facts. 'Not one thing or another, but in some ways both. Like frogs or newts or salamanders.'

'Ssssalamanders?'

Bennett nodded. 'You're keeping the hiss?'

'It ssssuits me,' the Serpent told him.

'Are your sure you really want to go?' Florizella asked. 'And leave us?"

'Weave me?' came a little whisper.

'A visit,' the Sea Serpent decided. 'A short ssstay only. I take it that this is a travelling show?' It turned to the Countess N'Asty. 'We will sssee the world?'

'You will,' she promised. 'And the world will see you. You will be one of the stars of the show.'

'I am extraordinarily vain,' the Sea Serpent agreed. 'You have a tank that is sssuitable? And you will feed me?' It slid a little sideways glance at Florizella and winked at the queen. 'You will feed me nice things to eat? Tasssty little morsssels? Perhaps now and then a pretty girl tied to a ssstake?'

'You promised not to do that any more,' the queen said sharply.

'You'll be well fed,' the countess assured it. 'And you will have a beautiful tank.'

'I'll come,' the Sea Serpent decided.

'As you like,' the king said cheerfully. 'And what about the Mammoth? D'you want him too?'

'Not the Mammoth!' Florizella cried.

'Is that what you call a mammoth. trying to hide behind the trees, but doing a very bad job?' the Countess N'Asty asked.

'Pwactically invisible!' came the little voice.

Florizella looked round and saw that the Mammoth was kneeling down so that he could cover his eyes with his giant feet, believing that if he couldn't see the Countess N'Asty, then she couldn't see him.

'I can see you perfectly well,' the countess told him scornfully. 'But you are neither Rare nor Disagreeable and I have no interest in you. You are common and pleasant, and I dislike both.'

'Compwete wobbwedewook!' came the muffled, defiant cry.

'He can stay here,' Florizella interrupted quickly. To her mother and father she said, 'He won't play Grandmother's Footsteps on his own.'

'No one to pway with?' the little voice said sadly.

'We will play with you,' Bennett promised kindly. 'But not on the drawbridge.'

'That's settled then,' the king said cheerfully.

'What about the yellow wolf?' the countess asked suddenly. 'I'll take him.'

Samson, who had been sitting in front of the king, giving the carriage cats a long, hard look, suddenly remembered that he had something urgent to do in the palace and trotted back inside.

'He's a dog,' the king said at once. 'A yellow dog.

Yellow but not rare. And never disagreeable.'

'Looks like a wolf to me,' the countess said. 'A wolf that someone has dyed yellow. That makes him pretty rare. And, if he lived with me for long enough, he would grow to be disagreeable.'

'He's a pet,' Florizella said firmly.

'He's ours,' Bennett agreed.

'He's not for collecting,' Courier told her.

Before the countess could argue, they heard the sound of wheels on the road and another cart came swaying through the trees towards the palace. It was pulled by two extremely large ginger cats, and it held a giant fish tank with coloured sand in the bottom and a little treasure chest sitting beside the fake waterweed.

'Your travelling tank,' the countess said to

the Sea Serpent. 'You'll have a bigger one at the show.'

'I'll do it!' the Sea Serpent exclaimed, and it slithered out of the moat, up the wheels of the cart, grasping with its strong forelegs and slithering with its long, scaly tail. Soon it was completely coiled up in the tank with its beautiful blue eyes looking out through the glass at Florizella, Bennett and Courier.

'Gosh,' Courier said. 'Are you sure?'

'Is there room for all of you?' Bennett asked.

'D'you really want to go?' Florizella whispered.

'Won't you miss me?' came a little voice from the orchard. The Mammoth raised his head for a moment to look at his friend in the travelling case, looped round and around like a coiled rope in a glass jar.

'Drive on!' the Sea Serpent commanded the countess, ignoring them all. 'To fame and fortune!'

She cracked her whip and the cats got to their feet and wandered off, the carriage bouncing and jolting behind them as they went first one way, then another, their tails waving, doing exactly what they wanted to do, though the countess hauled on the reins and shouted instructions. But – as they remarked to one another – nobody tells a cat what to do.

CHAPTER FIVE

*The Sea Serpent finds
something important in
its new life. It's sssignificant*

$\mathcal{J}$n the days that followed, Courier, Bennett, and Princess Florizella included the Mammoth in all their games, and even created some new ones especially for him, for fear of him missing his dear friend, the Sea Serpent. But it is very hard for a Mammoth to shine in playground games. Hide and Seek is quite impossible for a large Mammoth to win, unless played in a huge field with haystacks, and even then, what with a trunk at one end and a large bottom at the other, it is rather obvious when a Mammoth is hiding behind a haystack.

Tag is difficult too because, though Mammoths are eager, and this one was a fun-loving creature, they are not quick on their broad flat feet, and they can't dodge at all. Leapfrog is just dangerous for their playmates, and when the four of them tried Musical Bumps, it rocked the whole palace. But Musical Statues! The Mammoth was brilliant at Musical Statues, and his skill at Grandmother's Footsteps got better and better every day. He was always the last to move in Musical Statues and the first to get to the finish line when he played Grandmother's Footsteps. He could sneak up and freeze in a moment. He always won.

The Mammoth spent a lot of his time at the seaside where he helped the lifeguard make sure that swimmers did not go into deep water. Once, he performed a heroic rescue, tiptoeing out further and further with his trunk raised above the waves so that he could breathe while walking on the ocean floor. When he could see the legs of the boy splashing but sinking in the water, he came up underneath him like a submarine and the boy rode back to shore, standing on the Mammoth's submerged head, the trunk raised high before them, like a periscope on a submarine.

The Mammoth liked to help raise parasols and arrange deckchairs. Sometimes he gave rides and played games; but he never heard from his old friend. He never heard from the Sea Serpent. Nobody ever received a letter from it – not a postcard, not a message from a parrot, no word at all to say if it liked its new life in show business, or that it missed its friends.

'It doesn't phone?' the Mammoth asked Florizella.

'We don't have phones,' she reminded him.

'It doesn't wite?'

She shook her head. 'It doesn't write.'

'Do you miss it?'

'A bit,' she said. 'Do you?'

The Mammoth bowed his head and one large tear rolled down the fluffy ginger trunk. 'Vewy much.'

'Shall we go and visit it?' Florizella asked helpfully, patting an enormous leg.

The Mammoth shook his head. 'Too fwightening,' he said. 'The cwoss wady was too fwightening for me. But it wikes her. She is its new best fwend?'

'I suppose so,' Florizella agreed.

Apparently, the Sea Serpent had become the star of the show. Everyone in the kingdom — and everyone in all the neighbouring kingdoms — had heard of the Countess N'Asty's Rare and Disagreeable Show. Lots of people bought

tickets and went to see it. In a very short while, it became known simply as 'the Nasty Show', a title that would only please someone as unpleasant as the countess – she took it as a compliment.

It started with a display of things that were rare or unusual, just out of place or contradictory. There was a cage of hyenas, but none of them were laughing. You could win a prize (it was something quite horrible) if you told a joke so funny that it made the hyenas laugh. The next cage housed a kookaburra and it didn't laugh, either; it just looked down its beak in a really sulky way. Next door to these creatures was a spectacled bear with perfectly good eyesight, a rattlesnake without a rattle, a perfectly sensible raspberry crazy ant, a songbird without a tune, a lark with no sense of fun and a skunk with a light floral perfume. There was a good-tempered camel that never got the hump, a calling bird who never visited anyone, a nightingale who slept all night, and a screaming hairy armadillo that was completely bald and totally silent. Nothing lived up to its name except the star of the show in a large tank filled to the brim with crystal-clear water: the Sea Serpent.

The Countess N'Asty sold viewing tickets for the Sea Serpent , and a visitor could pay a fee to look at it through the glass. Sometimes the Sea Serpent would look back with its wide, cold gaze and all the naughty children would hammer on the thick glass and shout at it as it swam past. It always ignored them completely.

Sometimes it would pull itself out of the pool to lie on a beach, which made all the naughty children hammer on the glass and shout even louder. It always ignored them completely then too. Either way: in the water or out of it, on the beach or leaning against the fake cliffs the Sea Serpent got more and more bored and unhappy, and the children got noisier.

The Countess N'Asty also sold what she called 'lucky tickets'. People paid extra to see the Sea Serpent's feeding time, and the tickets were all put into the Countess N'Asty's hat. She herself drew out the winning ticket – and the prize was *to actually be the Sea Serpent's lunch*!

Yes! When the Countess N'Asty said she had a Nasty Show, she wasn't kidding. The holder of the winning lucky ticket was taken behind the Sea Serpent's glass cage, dressed up in a princess gown, wig and hat, and helped (sometimes rather *pushed)* through the door at the back of the cage, up the stairs inside the fake cliffs, and finally tied to a princess stake on a lump of fake rock at the back of the tank.

The Sea Serpent swam round and round the tank, getting faster and faster, and then – *WHOOSH!* – it would spring up to the pretend cliff and snap at the fake princess. *BANG!* At the same time it pressed a hidden lever in the rock and – *SWOOP* – down went the pretend princess into a hidey-hole in the middle of the fake cliffs as the Sea Serpent swam round and round in the water, pretending to be gulping down princess, careful to leave a little trail of pink princess veil coming out of its mouth.

Backstage, Countess N'Asty opened the door in the back of the tank and the winner slipped out – a little damp and always terrified. Once or twice the lucky ticket holder had been sick with fear, two of them had fainted and been slapped by the Countess N'Asty to make them feel better. Waiting for a Sea Serpent to eat you is very scary – even if it is an experience you have won. Most people wished they hadn't been so lucky on that day. Waiting while the Sea Serpent swam round and round was bad, but trusting that the Sea Serpent would press the lever to drop you into the hiding place was even worse.

This fake swallowing was troubling the Sea Serpent too. 'If I could eat just one, just once, I would feel ssso much better,' it said to the Countess N'Asty one evening as she was putting its picnic on a tray.

'I don't care how you feel,' she said frankly.

'You really are nasssty,' the Sea Serpent said with respect.

'I should certainly hope so,' she replied. 'You and I are the only things in this show that are what we say we are. Everyone else is a failure and a fraud.' She glanced at the cat that was accompanying her on her rounds, her security cat. 'And these are just brutes,' she said.

The cat snarled at her, showing its teeth.

'The thing is . . .' The Sea Serpent could not find the right words. It had a strange sensation, something like an ache, something that it had never known before. 'I am feeling sssomething,' it warned her. 'I am definitely feeling sssomething.'

The Countess N'Asty had no interest in this at all. She plonked the picnic tray down on the rock and turned to leave.

'I am feeling . . .' The Sea Serpent thought very long and hard. 'I am feeling An Emotion!'

'You are?' she paused. 'What sort of emotion?'

'What sssorts are there?' the Sea Serpent asked, quite bemused at itself. 'This is a sssort of ssstomach ache, and a hotness behind my eyes, and a sssort of downward tweak on my mouth. And I want a . . .' The Sea Serpent racked its brains. 'I think I want a hug,' it said, quite amazed at itself. 'Not a crushing squeeze.' It was struggling to understand what it was feeling. 'Not a boa-constrictor death hug. But a real hug. A loving hug. I have an ache inssside.'

'Indigestion, surely?' the countess asked.

'All I eat is the most boring of picnics,' it reminded her. 'No, this is definitely An Emotion. I can feel it! But what could it be?'

'There is happiness, sadness, disgust, fear, surprise and anger,' Countess N'Asty said briskly, ticking them off on her fingers, losing interest all the time, till by the time she got to 'anger' she was nearly out of the door.

'Is that all? Just sssix?'

'Those are the main ones, so they say.'

'And what do they feel like?'

'I don't know,' she said irritably. 'I've never felt any variety myself. I just always feel unpleasant, all of the time – not unpleasant for me, but unpleasant towards everyone else. I thought it was the same for you. You're supposed to be a cold-blooded reptile, aren't you? Solitary? Friendless? Frightening? That's why you're here in the Nasty Show!'

'I am an amphibian,' the Sea Serpent corrected her. 'But – agreed – I *am* nasty.' The Sea Serpent paused, two beautiful blue tears in its beautiful blue eyes. 'Or rather – I *was*!'

'So what are you now?' the countess asked crossly.

'I am feeling sssomething!' The Sea Serpent cried out, patting its slender stomach with its forelegs as if it were trying to find a lumpy emotion under its pearly green scales. 'I am feeling . . .' Clearly, this was the first emotion that it had ever felt and it was struggling to name it. 'It is sssadness!' it announced, horrified by the sensation, especially shocked that it – the perfect Sea Serpent – should feel anything worse than a stomach ache from eating a princess too quickly. Finally, it knew for sure: 'Countess N'Asty! I am feeling sssad! And I even know why! It is because I miss my friends.'

Countess N'Asty glared at the Sea Serpent. 'Well, that's too bad,' she said.

'Too bad? You are sssorry for me? I may feel a little better if my sssadness is understood.'

'No, no,' she said. 'I have no sympathy. I just mean it's too bad for you, too bad for them, of no interest to me. You're mine, you agreed to work here and, whether you're sad or happy, you're staying here and you're going to do the show and you're going to pretend to eat someone dressed up as a princess, every day, for the rest of your life.'

'For how long?' The Sea Serpent's beautifully shaped chin gave a little tremble. 'I thought I would ssstay here until I wanted to go home? Like now? Now that I want to go home?'

'Oh no,' said the countess with a mean smile. 'You're mine for life.'

CHAPTER SIX

*In which the Mammoth
too learns a great lesson.
(Really, I am quite impressed
with myself: this story is
becoming highly moral!)*

*B*ack at the beach, the Mammoth was building a solitary sandcastle. Sadly, he put a little flag in the single turret.

'Are you all right?' Florizella and Bennett came to admire the castle.

'Nice work,' Bennett said.

'It's the Sea Serpent's own fwag,' the Mammoth said.

'It had it's own flag?' Florizella asked.

'A half-eaten pwincess,' the Mammoth replied. 'On a stake, over a wave.'

'Nice,' Florizella said politely if not completely truthfully.

'We used to pway together,' the Mammoth said, sitting back on his plump back legs and looking at the castle.

'Pray?' Bennett asked, bewildered.

'Play,' Florizella explained. 'He's missing the Sea Serpent. And we've not heard from it. We don't know how it is at all. But he won't go to the Nasty Show to see it.'

'I can't bear to wook!' the Mammoth explained. 'Not at a Nasty Show. It hasn't asked us to go.'

'We'd come with you,' Bennett offered.

'No.' The Mammoth quickly refused. 'Not if

it doesn't want us.. 'It's not good manners.'

'DON'T SAY THAT!' Florizella shouted as two enormous Good Manner Eagles came screaming down from the sky, their giant wings blowing sand over everyone, landing beside Bennett and Florizella and glaring at them with their stern yellow eyes.

'Not good manners?' one asked at once. 'Did someone say you were planning to do something that was not good-mannered?'

'It was a perfectly polite visit to the Sea Serpent at the Nasty Show,' Bennett explained. 'We'd buy a ticket and we'd queue. We'd sit in the right seats and applaud when appropriate. Nothing bad-mannered at all.'

'Now that is a person who is *really* bad-mannered,' the other Good Manner Eagle observed. 'The Countess N'Asty. Rude.'

'Why don't you tell her?' Florizella demanded. 'Why don't you teach her to behave better? Instead of . . .' Florizella found that her sentence had disappeared as she realised it would be rude to say, 'always picking on us!' to a Good Manner Eagle.

'She is beyond help,' the first Good Manner Eagle ruled. 'Our job is to make sure that the young royals behave well. Especially princesses. Especially you. After all—' It paused and then the two of them chanted together, in perfect harmony:

'Politeness is a princess's greatest gift!'

'Yes,' Florizella said through gritted teeth. 'I know. You've said so. Often.'

'But not princes?' Bennett teased.

'Not Mammoths?' asked the Mammoth, joining in.

'The greatest gifts of a prince are generosity and kindness,' the Good Manner Eagle said sternly to Bennett. 'Of those to whom much is given, much is expected.'

'Come again?' Bennett asked.

'If you are born with everything handed to you on a plate (a golden plate, as it happens), and you have everything your own way, like a prince always does, then you're expected to give something back,' Florizella told him bluntly, still a bit irritated that princesses had to specialise in politeness.

'Fair enough,' Bennett said. 'That's why we gave up the Prince Permit – so that we didn't have everything our own way without giving something back. Us boys agreed it was unfair, and that girls should have a fair chance.'

'Yes, that's right,' Florizella said, feeling a bit happier.

'And Mammoths . . .' The Good Manner Eagle turned to the Mammoth, startling him with its stern look and big yellow beak.

'I don't do anything,' the Mammoth said quickly. 'I'm only wittle.'

'Wittle?' the Good Manner Eagle checked.

'Little,' Bennett and Florizella said together.

'Oh, but you do!' the Good Manner Eagle told the Mammoth. 'You have to learn to be brave.'

'Too wittle!' repeated the Mammoth piteously.

'You miss your friend,' the Good Manner Eagle explained. 'It misses you.'

'Weawwy?'

'It wants to come home to you, but it is trapped in a tank in the Nasty Show.'

'It can't wun away?'

'It can't. You have to find the courage to rescue it.'

'Wescue?'

'Wescue.' The Good Manner Eagle found the Mammoth's accent catching. Then it recovered itself. 'Its task is to learn that it has feelings. Like missing you. Your task is to find your courage.'

'Where do I find couwage?' The Mammoth's eyes were round with wonder.

'In your loving heart,' the Good Manner Eagle said gently. 'You have a gweat heart.'

'A gweat heart?' the Mammoth repeated in a whisper.

'Many wittle things have a gweat heart. You'll see.' Then the two Good Manner Eagles spread their shining white wings and sailed up into the sky without another word.

'Blimey,' said Bennett when he was sure that they were gone. 'This is a bit huge.'

'It's mammoth,' said Florizella.

They both turned to the Mammoth who had planted his head deep in the sandcastle, and put both his big front feet over his ears so that he could neither see nor hear the Good Manner Eagles and the great task they had put upon him.

CHAPTER SEVEN

Courier invents a
New Thing that may
be of no use at all. Over

The two royal children and the Mammoth went back to the palace to prepare for a great adventure. It took them a long time to get there for the Mammoth dawdled as much as he could, and at every road junction suggested that they go a longer way around. Finally, they got to the field outside the palace and found Courier shouting into an empty paper cup. A piece of string was stretched from the cup right across the field to another empty paper cup. A messenger parrot was standing on the rim of the cup with its little head right inside. When it came out, it looked very confused.

'That parrot looks like it doesn't understand a word that Courier is saying,' Bennett pointed out.

'They never understand,' Florizella pointed out. 'Hi, Courier, what are you doing?'

'I'm inventing,' he said. 'I have invented a telephone.'

'Gosh! Does it work?' Florizella asked.

'It doesn't work well with a parrot,' Courier said. 'And you weren't around so I couldn't try it on you.'

'Try me now,' Florizella offered, so Courier sent her to the other end of the field and pulled the string between the two cups so it was taut. He spoke into his paper cup while Florizella put her cup against her ear.

'Can you hear anything?' Bennett asked her.

'You know, it's amazing, but I can!' she said. 'But for some reason he's calling me Over.'

'Calling you over where?'

'Not over anywhere, just Over.'

Bennett put the cup to his ear. 'Oh, he's saying, "Can you hear me? Over!" Meaning that it's your turn to say something.' Bennett put the cup to his mouth and said, 'Yes, I can hear you. Over.'

'But why Over?' Florizella asked.

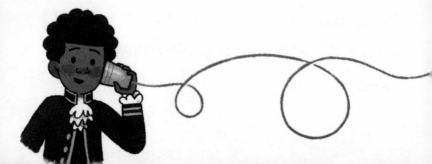

Bennett was listening intently.
'Now he's calling me Roger,'
he said.

He put the cup down and waved to Courier
to come back to their side of the field. 'Yes, it
works,' he said briefly as Courier joined them.
'But we don't have time for it right now. We
have to go and find the Sea Serpent.'

'That's what the parrot said.' Courier pointed
to the bird who had been helping him invent
the mobile phone. 'He's got a message.'

'You've got a message from the Sea Serpent?'
Bennett demanded. 'Why didn't you say so at
once? We've been waiting and waiting to hear
from it!'

'What's the message?' Florizella asked.

'Couldn't make it out,' Courier told her. 'Not on the mobile phone anyway.'

Florizella said nothing because there was a Good Manner Eagle circling high above them. If he had not been there, she might have said something very rude to her little brother. But she glanced up at the sky, glared at Courier and beckoned to the parrot.

It came at once and perched on her shoulder. 'Do you have a message?' Florizella asked nicely.

'For the Mammoth,' the parrot said clearly.

'Oh good,' Florizella said. 'Mammoth! This parrot has a message for you and it said your name really clearly, so maybe the message will be clear too.'

The Mammoth came closer to listen. They were all silent. The messenger parrot – this one was named Timothy – put its beautiful navy blue head on one side and said, 'I feel a notion, Missy Sue. Let's stew me.'

'Oh not again!' Bennett said.

Florizella shook her head. 'What?'

Timothy clicked his beak. 'I feel a notion, Missy Sue. Let's stew me.'

'You know, I really think my mobile phone is better than these parrots, over.' Courier said.

'You don't need to say "over" when you're not transmitting on your paper cup,' Bennett told him.

'It's a habit, over,' Courier said. 'I've got it now, and I can't stop, over.'

'What d'you think the parrot means?'

Florizella asked Bennett, completely ignoring Courier.

Bennett shrugged. 'Mammoth, do you know?'

'Did he say the Sea Serpent said not to wowwy about it, not to go to the Nasty Show, and that evewything's fine?' the Mammoth asked hopefully. 'And for me to just stay home?'

'I don't think so,' Florizella said. '"I feel a notion, Missy Sue" sounds like some sort of message. Bother. Now we'll have to go to the Nasty Show in case it's important.'

'But not meet the nasty wady,' the Mammoth urged. 'She doesn't wike me. She said so. She said I was common and pweasant.'

'We won't even see her,' Florizella reassured him. 'We'll just buy a ticket and whisper to the Sea Serpent when we see it.'

'We'll go disguised,' Bennett said. 'I'll wear a big hat.'

'Me too!' said the Mammoth, cheering up at the thought of dressing up.

'I'll wear a princess gown!' declared Courier. 'Over.'

'Over what?' Florizella demanded irritably.

'Over all of me,' Courier said smugly. 'A long one. Over.'

It is fair to say that the three children
and the Mammoth were as odd a sight
as any of the sideshows as they queued up,
very politely, at the Nasty Show gates. It was
a sunny afternoon in a green meadow, on the
border between Prince Bennett's Land of the
Deep Lakes, and Princess Florizella and Prince
Courier's Seven Kingdoms. Florizella had the
blue messenger parrot on her shoulder and

was wearing a green archer's costume with the pointy hat pulled low over her face. Bennett was dressed like a haymaker with an enormous floppy straw hat. He was carrying a pitchfork for extra effect, and Courier was dressed in full princess costume with the pointy hat called a henin on his blond curls.

The Mammoth had asked the royal hatter to make him a big cowboy hat. He was so afraid of the Countess N'Asty that he wore it low, pulled down over his eyes, believing that if he could not see her (or, indeed, anything) then she could not see him. This meant that the children had to stand on either side of him, two to steer him by his ears, and one behind to act as a brake by hauling on his tail. Since it was a Nasty Show there were quite horrible

people all around and nobody noticed them at all.

'Are you buying a ticket or selling him as an exhibit?' the ticket man asked pointing at the huge walking hat.

'No, no,' Florizella said. 'This is my . . . er . . . dog.'

'Bit big for a dog,' the man said, looking at the bobbing stetson and the huge russet body.

'Isn't he?' Courier agreed. 'That's what they all say. He's terribly big, even for a big dog. Over.'

'Rover, is he?' the man said, thinking Courier had said the dog's name.

'Rover,' Courier agreed as they shuffled past with the Mammoth between them. 'Over.'

'Come on, Rover-over,' Bennett said cheerily, pulling the Mammoth along, and they took their tickets and went in. Luckily, there was no turnstile where the Mammoth would have got stuck, but a double gate that Florizella opened wide.

They walked quickly past the cages of the sombre hyenas and the silent kookaburra bird. They could not bear to meet the eyes of the spectacled bear, or peer into the cage of the rattlesnake without a rattle or the grave raspberry crazy ant. Florizella turned her head from the aviary, which imprisoned the songbird without a tune, the lark with no sense of fun, the unsociable calling bird and the sleepy nightingale. Not even Courier admired the sweet-smelling skunk, the good-tempered camel or the silent and very bald screaming hairy armadillo.

'This is dweadful,' the Mammoth said, much distressed. 'Don't wet me go! Don't wet them take me too! Can't we go now? Will you wet me go home?'

'Soon,' Florizella said gently, and she and Bennett took a good grip of an ear each and Courier wrapped the Mammoth's tail round his hand as they turned a corner and saw the great glass tank. There, leaning on the sloping brim, looking bored and disdainful, was their old friend the Sea Serpent.

It saw them at once, and recognised them at once, but it did not call out. Its long green eyelashes closed in a wink and it leaned over the tank towards them.

'Hewwo! Huwwah! Hewwo!' the Mammoth cried out.

'Shhhh,' it said.

'We've come to see if you are all right,' Courier told it. 'Over.'

'Awwight!' the Mammoth gasped. 'Are you?'

'I'm not,' the Sea Serpent whispered. 'I want to come home.'

'Home?' the Mammoth piped.

'She won't let me leave.'

'Weave?'

The Sea Serpent sighed. 'Have I forgotten? Did he always repeat everything I said?'

'Wepeat!' the Mammoth repeated desperately.

'He's frightened,' Florizella explained. 'He's missed you, and he's frightened of Countess N'Asty.'

'Fwightened!' the Mammoth agreed, nodding furiously, his huge hat rocking on his head.

'Did you send a message asking for help?' Bennett asked.

'Yes,' the Sea Serpent said. 'It was that messenger parrot.' It pointed its long nose at the parrot Timothy who nodded emphatically, looking very pleased with himself.

'What did you say?' Courier asked. 'Over.'

The Sea Serpent leaned over the side of the tank so only they could hear it whisper. 'I sssaid: I feel Emotion,' it confided. It looked at them to see if they were surprised. They were completely stunned. The Sea Serpent nodded. 'I do! Really. Sssomething I have never felt before.'

The parrot nodded its blue head. 'I feel a notion,' it said.

'That's not right at all,' Courier told it. 'Over.'

The Sea Serpent turned its blue gaze on its friend, the Mammoth. 'I sssaid: I miss you.'

The Mammoth raised his head so that he could see the Sea Serpent from under the brim of his huge hat. 'I miss you too,' he whispered.

'Missy Sue!' the parrot confirmed. 'That's what I said: Missy Sue.'

'We've really got to find a better way of sending messages than these parrots,' Bennett said quietly to Florizella. 'They are worse than useless.'

'I asked for help,' the Sea Serpent told Florizella. 'I've never asked for help in my life before. I said: Ressscue me!'

Florizella gasped. 'That's not what we got at all. The parrot said: "Let's stew me."'

'The message made no sense at all,' Bennett said crossly. 'We had to come to see you to find out what you meant.'

'Compwete wobbwedewook!' the Mammoth contributed.

The Sea Serpent looked at the three royals and the enormous ginger Mammoth in their ridiculous hats. 'Would you rescue me?' it asked humbly. 'I know I have been . . . unpleasssant. But I have had time to think. I have become ssssensitive.'

The four fell silent. It was the Mammoth who spoke for them all. 'We are your fwends,' he said simply. 'Fowever.'

'But how can we rescue you?' Bennett asked. 'Can you get out of the tank?'

'Not at the front, but there is a door at the

back, if you could find the key,' the Sea Serpent suggested. 'Then, if you could help me reach the river, I could ssswim from there to the sssea.'

'Wescue,' the Mammoth repeated fearfully. 'Wiver.'

'She keeps the keys on a chain at her waist. She puts them under her pillow when she sssleeps. You'd have to go into her tent and sssteal them.'

'We can't do that,' the Mammoth said quickly. 'She'd be cwoss.'

'We might have a go,' Courier said. 'Over.'

'Does she sleep very heavily?' Florizella asked, thinking of fairytale rescues and escapes.

'We need some terrific sort of spell,' Courier

said. 'To make her sleep. Over.'

'That's it!' Florizella said. 'A sleepover! Genius.'

'I thought I was,' Courier said, quite pleased. 'But why? Over.'

'A sleepover! We'll ask her if one of us can have a sleepover with her. And then steal the keys.'

'One of you,' the Mammoth agreed hastily. 'Not someone wittle.'

'Yes,' Bennett said. 'Probably Courier, as he was nice to her when she came to the palace, and it's his brilliant idea. And then we can rescue him when it all goes wrong.'

'When it goes wrong?' Courier repeated. 'You said "when". Over.'

'I meant if it goes wrong,' Bennett corrected himself.

'But why would she invite him?' Florizella was interrupted by a drum roll and a flash and a *BANG!* and the Sea Serpent hissed crossly. It slid down into the water of the tank as the Countess N'Asty suddenly appeared on the rock that overhung the water, standing next to something that looked very like a princess stake.

The royal children and the Mammoth hurried to the back row of seats and ducked down low so that the countess did not notice them as she bellowed at the audience.

'LADIES AND GENTLEMEN, BOYS and GIRLS, ANYONE and EVERYONE – welcome to the nastiest, most brutal show on earth!

Here you see the most savage and ferocious creature, captured from its native waters and brought here to you at TREMENDOUS expense and danger – the Sea Serpent!'

The Sea Serpent swam a couple of laps round the tank and snarled at the children who were thumping on the glass.

'You know that noise goes ssstraight through my head,' it told them. 'Don't tap on the glass! Don't ever tap on anybody's glass. It's the worst thing you can do.'

'It is feeding time for this savage creature!' the countess bellowed. 'And this monster likes nothing better than to eat a beautiful princess!'

'Ooooh!' said everyone in the audience.

The three royals looked rather uncomfortable, especially Florizella, who was a genuine princess, but was dressed up today like Robin Hood. It was even worse for Courier who was dressed – rather unfortunately he now thought – as a proper fairytale princess, in full pink robe, ruffles and pointy hat.

'Luckily, in the audience today, we have a visiting princess!' yelled the countess. She had spotted Courier at the start of the show. 'Stand up, Your Royal Highness, and take a bow!'

Everyone was looking at Courier. The people who had the lucky tickets were beaming at him – really glad, now that they had seen the Sea Serpent, that it was Courier who was the lucky one.

'This is your big chance,' Bennett told him quickly. 'Go and do whatever trick they want and then ask her if you can stay to dinner, make friends, wait for her to fall asleep and then steal the keys and rescue the Sea Serpent.'

'Or wun away,' the Mammoth whispered down its trunk. 'I would.'

Two strong tabby cats obeying the Countess N'Asty's nod, came round the bank of seats, took tight hold of Courier and led him to the front so that everyone could see him.

'What's your name, dearie?' the countess demanded, sickeningly sweet.

'Courier, over,' Courier said in a very small voice.

'Princess Courier-Over, you are going to go into the tank with this fearsome creature! Do you dare?'

Courier, a little pale, nodded. Of course, he had done this once before, but last time

Florizella and Bennett were standing by, swords drawn, ready to fight the Sea Serpent. Now he was in the grip of Countess N'Asty, and the Sea Serpent had been bored and hungry for weeks.

The Mammoth had pulled his Stetson hat down low over his eyes – he couldn't bear to watch. 'Don't do it!' he whispered, too afraid to speak clearly. Bennett chewed anxiously on a stalk of straw. Florizella stepped a little closer to the tank as if to remind the Sea Serpent of the important difference between a rescue party and lunch.

Courier was led round to the back of the tank. There was the noise of a key grating in a lock as the cats opened the cage and pushed him up the ladder. Then suddenly Courier appeared beside the countess on top of the rock in the tank with the Sea Serpent swimming around in the water beneath them.

'I shall tie the princess to the stake!' the countess told the audience.

'Tie her to the stake!' everyone said.

'The Sea Serpent will approach her!'

'The Sea Serpent will approach her!'

'And SNAP! With one bite, it will eat her up!'

'Eat her up!' everyone cried. 'Eat her up!'

'I can't bear to wook!' the Mammoth moaned. 'I can't!'

Courier, rather pale under his beautiful hat, was tied to the stake. He glanced over at his friends. The Mammoth was wide-eyed

and looked simply terrified. Florizella and Bennett nodded vigorously, to reassure him that everything was going well. Courier was not at all convinced.

'The Sea Serpent won't actually eat Courier, will it?' Bennett checked with Florizella. 'This is a trick, right? It does it every day and it can't eat people in a public show. It's just pretend. It will remember that we're here to rescue it?'

Florizella was worried. 'It ought to remember. But it does love a royal. It has very loyal tastes.'

The Sea Serpent was swimming faster and faster, round and round the tank, making the water frothy with its incredible speed. The countess stepped back out of sight. Courier was alone at the stake, his lips silently forming the words, 'Eject. Eject. Over!' when, with a great tidal wave of green water, the Sea Serpent lurched towards him and snapped its big white teeth. Courier flinched, but he could not get away from those gaping jaws.

'I can't wook! I can't bear to wook!' the Mammoth moaned.

'Sea Serpent! No!' Florizella shouted, quite appalled at the terrible sight. Then – there was a horrible silence and it was all over, Courier was gone, and the Sea Serpent was swimming slowly, lazily, round and round in the tank, smiling as if it were satisfied with a full tummy. Coming from its mouth was a trail of pink ribbon.

CHAPTER NINE

*In which a great deal
happens, but Courier,
once again, identifies
the 'main thing'*

In the underground cavern beneath the trapdoor, Countess N'Asty was untying Courier from the stake. His hat had been bitten in half, and his golden curls were damp. He was white with shock.

'You did very well,' she said. 'Most people faint.'

'Thank you,' Courier said. He did not say 'over' at the end of every sentence. He had been

cured of the 'overs' by the tremendous fright –
just like someone can be cured of hiccups.

'You can have a free ticket to come to the
show again,' she said. 'Bring a friend.'

'Thank you,' he said feebly.

'You can come in for free if you wear the
princess gown,' she offered. 'You can be eaten
again.'

Courier shook his head. He was quite sure
he did not ever want to be that close to being
eaten again. 'What I would really like would be
to stay behind when everything shuts up for
the night,' he said. 'If I might.'

'Why?'

'I admire you so much,' Courier said, lying
madly. 'I'd like to go around with you and close
up the show, help you put the animals to bed.

I'd like to hang out with you in the evening. Perhaps I could stay for a sleepover?'

'This is unusual,' the countess said suspiciously, she had never had a sleepover in her life, because everyone hated her. 'Don't you have to ask your mother?'

'I'm allowed,' Courier said, 'because it is Fairytale Land. May I stay?'

'You want a sleepover?' the countess confirmed. 'With me?'

'Yes,' he said bravely. But, with the countess glaring at him with her mean little eyes, he was not so sure that he did.

'You know my bedroom is small and dark and smelly, right?' she asked.

'Charming,' Courier said. 'Simple. Just like mine.'

'You know it's a dirty old tent?'

'Not a problem.'

'And the carriage cats sleep in my bed?'

'I love cats,' he lied.

'All right,' she said begrudgingly. 'Didn't you come with some people? A funny-looking green elf, and a walking scarecrow and an enormous dog in a hat?'

'Yes,' Courier said, pleased that their disguises had worked so well. 'I'll go and tell them to set off home without me. Then I'll come to your tent.'

The closing bell started to ring. 'Go on then,' Countess N'Asty said. 'And make sure everyone leaves. I don't want anyone else cluttering up my Nasty Show. No extra nasties. And no nice people at all. You can only stay for one night, remember. And don't be pleasant at breakfast.'

'Right away,' Courier said, and ran to find the others.

They were waiting by the exit gate.

'I've got in!' Courier said excitedly. 'Make it look as if you are leaving, but hide behind the cages, in that little wood over there. I'll come for you as soon as I've got the keys and then we can get the Sea Serpent out of the tank and into the river.'

'And I've got a sleeping spell for Countess N'Asty,' Florizella said.

'That was quick.'

'I called an enchanter,' she confessed. 'He

dropped it from a balloon. Bennett caught it. Here it is.'

Bennett handed the pouch of sparkly dust to Florizella and she passed it to Courier.

'Be careful,' she said. 'The bag split as he dropped it.'

Sure enough, as she handed it over, the purse of sleeping dust broke open and a cloud rose into the air. All the children breathed it in. Only the Mammoth, whose trunk was coiled away, did not get so much as a sniff of it.

'Does this work?' Bennett asked. 'Because I can smell it, but I'm not at all sleepy.'

'You need a lot,' Florizella said. 'Blow the whole purse over her, Courier, or sprinkle it on her pillow.'

'We'll wait for you here,' Bennett promised.

'Come and find us as soon as she's asleep. Good luck.'

'Shouldn't I wait for you at the pawace?' the Mammoth offered. 'Wather than here?'

'You remember what the Good Manner Eagle said,' Bennett told him. 'You have to find your great heart. This is your chance. Stay here with us and you can help rescue our friend.'

'But I'm too wittle' the Mammoth objected. 'And vewy easily fwightened.'

But Courier was already gone, with the purse of sleeping dust held tightly in his hand.

'Let's go into hiding,' Bennett said to Florizella.

She led the way to the wood behind the animal cages and sat down beneath a spreading oak tree. Bennett settled down next to her, the

Mammoth beside him, and they leaned against the tree trunk, looking up at the sky through the leaves.

'We keep watch,' Bennett said. 'We stay alert.'

'The stars are coming out,' Florizella remarked. 'Isn't it lovely?'

'It's cosy here,' Bennett said.

'Mmm. Doesn't it make you feel sss . . . llll . . . eee . . . ppp . . .y?'

'Not at all,' Bennett said.

And, in a moment, both children were fast asleep.

The Countess N'Asty's was ready for sleep as well in her damp and ragged tent. She had made a little bed for Courier out of old curtains and pillows, and she was already tucked up in her bed with both of the enormous black cats. Courier tipped the whole purse of sleeping dust into his hand and blew it towards the three of them. It rose in a cloud and settled gently over the whole tent, the countess, the cats and . . . Courier. Within moments, they were all sleeping as soundly in the tent as Bennett and Florizella in the little wood.

Only the Mammoth, who had not breathed in the sleeping dust, was awake. Like a sentry on night watch, he saw the moon come up, he heard the hoot of the owl and, though he listened hard for anything else, he heard nothing. Quietly, he rose to his feet and, with his trunk, he gently lifted the pointed archer's hat from Florizella's face. She did not stir. The Mammoth rolled Bennett over, so the boy was on his back. At once, he started to snore.

'Wake up!' the Mammoth whispered. 'You've got to wescue . . .' But neither child moved at all, except Florizella, who rolled over on her side, smiling at her dreams.

'Wake!' the Mammoth said more urgently, but nobody did.

'Oh dear! Oh dear! Oh dear!' the Mammoth said. 'Who is going to wescue the Sea Serpent?' He thought for a moment. 'My fwend the Sea Serpent who misses me.' For a minute, he stood as still as a mammoth statue as thoughts passed slowly through his big brain. 'Couwier,' he decided. 'He will get the keys from the nasty wady when she's asweep. I shall help him.' He thought for a moment. 'But I won't get too cwose,' he decided. 'And if she is awake and angwy I shall cweep away and hide.'

Leaving the two sleeping royals, he crossed the moonlit meadow towards the Countess N'Asty's tent. The animals in the Nasty Show watched him go, but none of them made a sound. They all wanted to know what would happen next. Not one of them thought that the Mammoth would be brave enough to make it as far as the Countess N'Asty's tent.

'Care to take a bet?' the cheerful camel asked. 'I reckon he'll not even lift the tent flap.'

The spectacled bear said nothing, but that was only because he never said anything. He didn't think the Mammoth's courage would last as far as the tent pegs, never mind opening the door.

And indeed, the Mammoth paused a long way off, hoping to see Courier creep out with the bunch of keys in his hand.

The Nasty Show was completely quiet, completely still. So was the tent. Nothing happened.

'I can't go any cwoser,' the Mammoth reminded himself. 'I'm not bwave wike Couwier.' He waited a few minutes more. 'I just can't,' he said.

The moon shone down on the meadow. Bennett and Florizella slept in the wood. Courier and Countess N'Asty slept in the tent. The Sea Serpent, feeling a new sensation that it recognised as an emotion – hope – waited for rescue. It felt certain that its friends would not fail it. The Mammoth waited patiently for someone else to do something.

Nobody did.

Slowly, in the Mammoth's large brain an idea was forming. First, he realised that this was the perfect opportunity, probably the one and only opportunity for a rescue, and that someone should take it.

Then, he realised that nobody was awake but himself and the Sea Serpent. If anyone was going to rescue the Sea Serpent tonight, it would have to be him. If he didn't do it now, there might never be another chance.

Then, he thought that he was too young and too frightened to face up to the Countess N'Asty. What if she was not asleep but only foxing? What if she rose up and grabbed him and shouted at him? For a moment, he froze in fright at the thought of her, and his furry knees trembled.

But then he remembered that he would dare almost anything for his friend the Sea Serpent. His friend who played with him . . . those great games of Grandmother's Footsteps! Those long sunny afternoons when he crept along the drawbridge and learned to walk so silently that he was hardly ever caught . . .

Slowly, the Mammoth raised his head and straightened his cowboy hat. He knew he was a master of the stealthy tread, an expert in the quick freeze. So that was what he was going to do! He was going to creep up to Countess N'Asty, just like he did in Grandmother's

Footsteps. He was going to sidle like a silent ninja into her tent, slide his trunk under her pillow, and feel for the keys to the Sea Serpent's tank with the wonderfully sensitive tip of his trunk. Then he would draw the keys, with not one chink, out from under her pillow . . . and escape!

CHAPTER TEN

'Wove made me bwave'

*J*ust as he used to do on the palace drawbridge, the Mammoth started his stealthy approach. *PAD . . . PAD . . . PAD.* That brought him to the outstretched ropes of the tent. Daintily, he stepped over them and untied the tent door. *Shuffle . . . shuffle . . .* That took him halfway into the doorway. Bowing low, so that he did not brush the roof, he took one cautious step over the sleeping

Prince Courier and poised silently, on his fluffy tiptoes, to slide his trunk under the Countess N'Asty's pillow.

She stirred in her sleep and the Mammoth went rigid. His heart was beating so loudly that he thought the thudding noise would wake her, but still he did not turn and run. Not even now, not at the worst moment, did his courage fail him. One huge black cat, asleep on the pillow, opened its green eyes, found it was nose to nose with a ginger mammoth, and closed them again, thinking it was a ridiculous dream. In a grumbly purr, it muttered to itself that it had better lay off the pilchards. The countess did not wake.

Silently, the acclaimed master of Grandmother's Footsteps drew the keys from underneath the pillow and held them tightly in his trunk. Now he had to do something that was yet more skilful. There was no room to turn in the tent so he would have to back out the way he had come in, making no noise. Keeping his little eyes fixed on the sleeping countess, the Mammoth went in reverse. Silently, he tiptoed backwards to the door, stepping carefully over Courier in his little bed, all the way to the tent doorway. His huge ginger bottom brushed the flap open, and he felt the meadow grass under his back feet. Amazingly, he had made it out.

But he did not run away. He leaned back into the tent, took a firm grip of the train of Courier's pink princess gown and pulled him from his bed, and out of the tent.

Courier slept on, dragged step by step through the meadow grass, over the bumpy ruts of the lane, all the way to the Sea Serpent tank.

'What have you got there?' The Sea Serpent

swam up to the glass and peered over the top. 'Looks like dinner.'

'It's Pwince Couwier,' the Mammoth whispered. 'Asweep. They're aww asweep. I had to do evewything on my own!'

'You got the keys?' The Sea Serpent was amazed. 'All on your own?'

'Aww by myself!' the Mammoth exulted, still in a hushed voice. 'I was bwave!'

'However did you dare?' The Sea Serpent knew its friend was afraid of almost everything, and nervous about the rest.

The Mammoth shook his head. Truly, he did not know. His love for his friend had been greater than his fear.

'Let me out!' the Sea Serpent exclaimed. 'Quick!'

The Mammoth left Courier where he was lying and galloped on his tip toes round to the back of the tank. The keyhole was awkward and he had to find the right key and then turn it. There was a screech of metal as the key turned and the Mammoth held his breath in case anyone heard it. At once, the kookaburra let out a call, the first laugh that had ever pealed out in the Nasty Show, just to cover the noise of the turning key and the shooting of the bolts.

Inside the tank, the Sea Serpent swam up to the fake cliff and pressed on the lever, the princess stake dropped into the dry chamber below and the Sea Serpent, fluid as a snake, climbed the rock face and poured itself down into the gap into the chamber and out of the open door. It wrapped itself round the

Mammoth like a boa constrictor and gave him a huge hug. 'Thank you,' it said. Tears stood in its beautiful blue eyes. 'You are a true friend. A true, brave friend.'

'I am your fwend,' the Mammoth said proudly. 'Wove made me bwave.'

'Now let's get out of here.' The Sea Serpent was still new to emotions and found them tiring. It started off, crawling with its forelegs and slithering with its tail.

'We have to bwing him!' The Mammoth went round to the front of the tank, where Courier lay like Sleeping Beauty in his pink princess dress, fast asleep in the moonlight.

'Do we?' the Sea Serpent asked carelessly, coming up beside the Mammoth. 'You mean in case we get hungry?'

'No!' the Mammoth exclaimed, quite shocked. 'Because he is your fwend too.'

'Him as well?' the Sea Serpent exclaimed, feeling rather overburdened by the love of others. 'What about Florizella and Bennett?'

'We have to get them as well. They're asweep.

We can't weave them there.'

'Sssurely they'll be OK,' the Sea Serpent started. 'The worst thing she can do is put them in a tank.'

The Mammoth looked at it. 'Don't you want to save them? Don't you wike them?' he asked. 'Don't you wove them?'

There was a long, awkward moment. No one had asked the Sea Serpent such a question ever before. It wasn't even sure if Sea Serpents could love people. The beautiful, strange creature and the fluffy Mammoth looked at each other, and they saw truly into each other's brave, loving hearts.

'I do,' said the Sea Serpent. 'I wouldn't have thought it, but I really do.'

'You don't want to eat him?' The Mammoth

pointed his trunk at Courier, knowing this was the greatest test.

'I don't,' the Sea Serpent said. 'I want to rescue him.' Inspired by real affection, it wrapped a coil round Courier and set off, dragging him along, towards the exit gate.

Very soon they came upon Florizella and Bennett, slowly stirring and getting to their feet.

'Oh wow, is it all over?' Florizella asked. 'I thought I'd just dropped off for a minute, but is it all done?'

'I did it!' the Mammoth said delightedly. 'I was bwave. And the Sea Serpent wescued Couwier because it woves him.'

'It's going to eat him,' Bennett said pessimistically, shaking out his peasant smock and pulling on his big hat.

'No, no, it's weawwy got emotions,' the Mammoth said earnestly. 'It can feel wove.'

'Come on then,' said Florizella. 'Let's get out of here before Countess N'Asty finds he's gone.'

Florizella and Bennett lifted Courier to his feet and dragged the sleeping prince towards the exit. Courier had breathed in far more sleeping dust than they had, so he was slower to wake. They opened the gate and were just about to go through it when the Sea Serpent, who had been dawdling at the back, said: 'Hang on a minute.'

'What?' Florizella demanded. Courier was a dead weight, and she was still sleepy. She wanted to get back to the palace as quickly as possible and be happy ever after. 'What now?'

'It's the other animals,' the Sea Serpent sounded puzzled. 'What about them?'

'Well, what about them?' Bennett yawned and he slumped against Courier who slumped against Florizella who staggered under their weight.

'I don't want to leave them in the show,' the Sea Serpent said. It spoke slowly as if it could hardly believe what it was saying. 'I would feel . . .' It put its foreleg to its pale scaly belly. 'I would feel sssomething bad.'

'Hunger?' asked Bennett.

'I would feel that I was in the wrong,' the Sea Serpent said thoughtfully. 'I've never felt that before. I think this is guilt that I am feeling. I think I would feel guilty if I left them.'

'Blimey!' Bennett said.

Florizella looked at the Sea Serpent with new respect. 'You're right,' she said. 'It would be wrong to rescue you and leave them. We must release them.'

'Wewease them?' the Mammoth whispered fearfully. 'But aren't they nasty? They are in the Nasty Show.'

'Surely they're just creatures that contradict their names,' Florizella said.

The Mammoth handed her the bunch of keys and she went along the cages, unlocking the doors and opening them. The sulky hyenas came silently out, looked around as if they could not believe their luck, and then melted into the darkness. A little experimental giggle echoed back to the rescuers. The kookaburra gave a chuckle and flew off. Bennett had to go into the cage and shake the spectacled bear to wake him up, but the rattlesnake slithered off, the raspberry crazy ant planned a careful route home, the songbird gave a little whistle as if it thought something might come of it, the lark flew off, looking for good times, and the skunk went quietly out, its tail carefully turned away from the rescuers. The camel, the calling bird, the nightingale and the silent and bald screaming hairy armadillo left together. Within moments, the only creature left was the spectacled bear that blinked at its rescuers and sat down heavily at their feet.

'Should we have released all these animals, just like that, into the wild?' Bennett asked. 'What if they don't settle?'

'It's Fairytale Land,' Florizella reminded him.

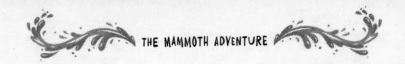

'Everyone is always happy ever after in the end.'

'I don't think the Countess N'Asty will be very happy when she finds everything is gone,' Courier pointed out. 'Hadn't we better get away before she wakes?'

'Yes!' said the Mammoth, alarmed at the thought. 'Huwwy.'

The children, the Mammoth, the Sea Serpent and the spectacled bear who thought it best to follow them in case this was all a dream that led to buns, left through the open exit gate and headed for the river. The Sea Serpent slithered into the cool water and swam downstream. The three children and the bear and the Mammoth walked along the grassy bank, keeping pace with it. Ahead of them they could see Florizella's palace, turrets gleaming in the early-morning sunshine. The river flowed into the deep moat and the Sea Serpent slid into its old place under the drawbridge with a sigh of relief.

'Home at lassst,' it said.

'And we can get some breakfast,' Courier said. The spectacled bear looked hopeful.

'And we can pway,' the Mammoth exclaimed.

As the Sea Serpent immediately coiled itself under the drawbridge, the Mammoth went back to the edge of the woods and started to creep forward. The bear, watching this with some surprise at first, quickly understood the game and started to creep too. *PAD-PAD-PAD* went the Mammoth's soft feet on the drawbridge. A little quieter but not far behind him came the bear, *pad . . . pad . . . pad*, then the *scuttle-scuttle-scuttle* of eight heavy feet and a *whoosh* as the Sea Serpent raised its head and said: 'You moved!'

The turret window above the drawbridge opened with a bang. The king put his head out, looked down at all the noise and said crossly: 'Oh no! Not again! Not again! They're back! And now there's a *bear* playing as well!'

Courier looked up at his father. 'We didn't bring the hyenas, Daddy-King,' he pointed out. 'Nor a screaming hairy armadillo. And surely that's the main thing.'

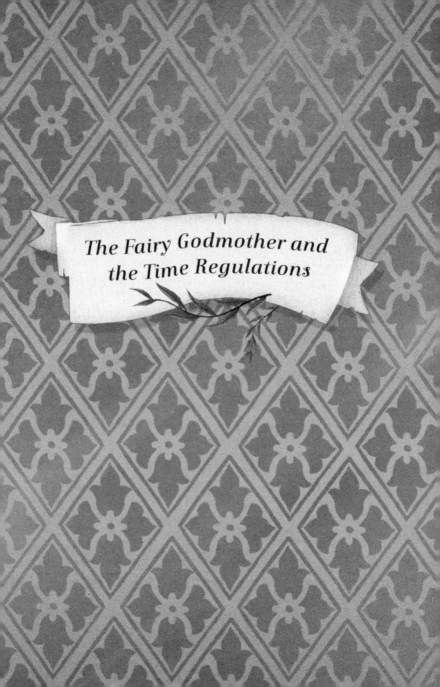

The Fairy Godmother and
the Time Regulations

CHAPTER ONE

*In which Florizella,
unfortunately, fails
as a friend*

rincess Florizella and her brother,
Prince Courier, were on their ponies,
leading the spectacled bear between them on
the winding path into the dark depths of the
Purple Forest. The bear wasn't really that
keen. He enjoyed his games and picnics at the
palace. He was not feeling at all feral. They
were not so much leading him as towing him
by his red leather collar. He was a big bear,

and they made very slow progress.

'This is hard work,' Courier complained. 'And pointless. As soon as we let him go, he's just going to come straight back to the palace.'

'Not if we introduce him to the forest and he sees he can be happy here,' Florizella insisted, looking rather doubtfully at the spectacled bear, who had taken advantage of the momentary halt to sit on his large fluffy bottom and suck his paws. 'Surely he wants to live in the wild and be free?'

'He isn't exactly racing us into the woods,' Courier pointed out. 'He's never said he wants to be free – has he?'

'He doesn't speak,' Florizella said. 'We have to just guess what he wants.'

'Sounds like you're guessing what *you* want,' Courier said.

Florizella thought that one of Courier's many irritating little habits – apart from constantly inventing things, apart from declaring what was the 'main thing', apart from arguing – was his ability to see the truth. What was worse is that he always, *always* said it out loud.

'Of course he would rather be free in the woods than playing Grandmother's Footsteps at the palace,' she said firmly.

Courier smiled at her. 'And – since that's what the parents want – we'd better get him deep into the Purple Forest and hope that he likes it.'

'He'll make friends with other bears,' Florizella said with less certainty. 'I'm sure wild bears are very friendly.'

'Of course he will.'

'And he'll eat . . . What will he eat?'

'Honey?' Courier suggested. 'Buns? What do they eat in the wild?'

Florizella got off her horse, Jellybean, tied him to a tree and sat down on a rock. She sighed. The bear sighed also, as if he too was tired of the long walk into the Purple Forest, though he had done very little walking and had been mostly heaved. Courier dismounted and stood beside the two of them.

'If Daddy King or Mummy Queen could only see how useful he would be, they'd let him stay,' Florizella said.

'How could he be useful? What do bears usually do in palaces?' Courier asked. 'I

thought they were generally found to be—' He broke off what he was saying and nodded at his sister, as if they shared a secret that could not be spoken.

'What?'

'You know . . .'

Courier spread his arms wide, as if he were trying to fly, and nodded again meaningfully.

'What are you doing now?'

Courier outretched, now, opened his mouth in a strange sort of snarl and closed his eyes.

'Sleepwalking?' Florizella guessed.

Courier opened his eyes and shook his head. He looked embarrassed. Then, as the bear sucked his paws without paying any attention, Courier lay down on his tummy on the forest floor, stretched out his arms again, spread out his legs, shut his eyes tight and opened his mouth in a broad, toothy grin. Now both the bear and Florizella stared in alarm.

'What are you doing?' Florizella asked.

'Rug!' Courier said in a hoarse whisper.

'What?'

'It's the only use I've ever seen anyone make of a bear in a palace,' Courier continued in his loud whisper. 'I'm sorry to say it, but the only bear I've ever seen in any palace was a bearskin rug.'

Florizella jumped up and put her hands over the bear's big fluffy ears to prevent him hearing any more. 'What a thing to say!' she said. 'How could you?'

Courier got up and quickly brushed leaves off his front. 'Sorry,' he said. 'I tried to mime it. It's tragic but true.'

'Better that he lives in the wild than becomes a rug!' Florizella exclaimed and, leading Jellybean with the reins in one hand and dragging the bear by his paw with the other, she started to walk deeper into the forest.

When they came to a small clearing a long way from the palace, Florizella turned to the bear. 'This is your new home,' she told him kindly. 'See, a lovely dry cave for your bedroom and for hibernation.'

'You do know about hibernation?' Courier checked.

The bear looked from one face to another and did not indicate by so much as the twitch of a whisker that he knew about hibernation or if he had observed his lovely dry cave.

'Well, anyway,' Florizella said, 'I'm sure

it will come to you naturally in winter. And there's a stream nearby where you can perhaps fish. And there will be bees making honey, and nuts and fruit, and lots of things to eat when you look around for them. But for now – here's a picnic lunch to start you off.'

'We're just going to unpack the picnic basket and leave you to it,' Courier said cheefully. 'Have a great time. It's – er – good to be wild, you know. I'm sure you'll like it.'

The two children opened the basket and spread out the food.

'What did you get him?' Courier asked quietly.

'His favourites,' Florizella said. 'Jelly and . . .' She had to blink away a tear. 'Fishpaste,' she said. 'He loves fishpaste sandwiches.'

'Odd,' said Courier. 'But perhaps they remind

him of salmon. Here,' he said to the bear. 'You can share these fishpaste sandwiches with your bear friends.'

Bear said nothing, as he always said nothing, and the two children opened all the little jars and boxes in the picnic hamper and stepped back. They waited until he took a sandwich, and then they led their ponies down the narrow path, not looking back, going faster all the time until the track widened and they could mount and trot home, hoping that the bear would eat his lunch and then have a little nap and wake up to being wild.

'That went quite well,' Courier said as they arrived, a few hours later, a little breathless, at the palace moat.

'Where's Bear?' the Mammoth asked at once.

The Sea Serpent slid the first half of its scaly body on to the grass at the side of the moat and looked at them with its beautiful blue eyes. 'Yesss,' it enquired. 'Where is Bear? And where is the picnic hamper? And why are you both ssso out of breath?'

Both children looked terrifically guilty.

'If I didn't know better, I would think you had eaten him,' the Sea Serpent observed. 'No hamper, no Bear, you two looking as if you have done sssomething dreadful.'

'We have done something dreadful!'

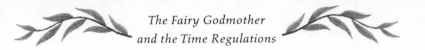

Although Florizella was a girl who rarely cried, the Sea Serpent's question struck her to the heart, and she burst into tears. 'Oh, Sea Serpent! We have done something dreadful!'

'Eaten him?' the Sea Serpent asked understandingly. 'It's easily done. A moment's inattention and old habits die hard. A little cuddle turns into a deadly sssqueeze and then a gulp, and it's all too late to sssay sssorry . . .'

'No!' said Courier, quite revolted. 'Of course we've not eaten him! But we have lost him.'

'Wost him?' The Mammoth looked painfully shocked. 'But he's so big. How could you woose him? Is he tewwifficawwy good at Hide and Seek?'

Florizella from one loving puzzled face to another and owned up. 'We lost him on purpose,' she said, and fell against the

Mammoth's soft side and cried.

The Mammoth was very comforting – he wrapped her up in his trunk and rocked her until she rubbed her tears away, and unrolled herself and said, 'I've let my friend down – the very worst thing you can do.'

'Oh, I don't know,' said the Sea Serpent thoughtfully. 'I can think of worsssse.'

'Like what?' Courier asked, guessing correctly that the Sea Serpent had done many bad things and never once cried over them.

The Sea Serpent smiled at him and licked its green lips. 'Better not asssk,' it advised him. 'Sssome accidents are better forgotten.'

'Forgotten and forgiven?' Courier checked.

'Nothing to forgive,' the Sea Serpent said smoothly. 'Or rather no one left to forgive.'

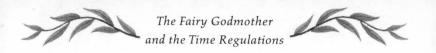

'Because they're . . . ?'

'Gone.' The Sea Serpent shrugged its shoulders, making its long, lean, green scaly body ripple. 'Alasss.'

'Alasss,' Courier said, trying out the word. 'Alasss.'

'Wost?' the Mammoth ignored all this in his worry for Bear.

'But what should I do?' Princess Florizella demanded. 'We were so sure he would like to live in the wild and now I don't know.'

'You wost our fwend?' Mammoth demanded.

'I know! I know! It was the wrong thing to do,' Florizella declared. 'I'll go straight back into the Purple Forest and find him.'

'That's not going to be easy,' Courier started. 'We went a long way, and the forest is full of robbers and wolves and brigands and bears. Of course, it's now one bear extra. Why don't we wait a few days, give him a chance to settle in, and then go with the captain of the guard and some soldiers to see if he's OK?'

Florizella shook her head. 'Not another moment,' she said. 'I'm not leaving him there on his own overnight. I'm going now. And if none of you want to come with me – you don't have to.'

'I *could* come,' the Mammoth said in a voice so quiet that Florizella did not even hear the brave offer.

'Oh! Nobody!' she said.

'Mammoth said he would,' said Courier. 'And I will too – as I said, in two days' time, with the guard.'

'Why not now?' Florizella was secretly a little

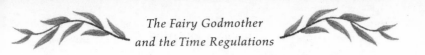

afraid of the Purple Forest as night fell and the robbers and wolves and brigands and bears (now one extra) came out of their daytime hideaways and looked for jelly, and fishpaste sandwiches, lonely travellers and princesses, or whatever else they fancied.

'You'll need backup,' Courier said cleverly. 'You go now, and me and Mammoth and Sea Serpent will be ready if you need us. You know - if we had a telephone, you could call us.'

'I'll take a messenger parrot,' Florizella decided.

'Alasss,' Courier said, liking the word more and more. 'Alasss.'

CHAPTER TWO

*In which the
messenger parrot
proves its worth again*

*F*lorizella saddled up Jellybean again.
He was most reluctant to set off to the
Purple Forest for the second time that day.
Jellybean was not very keen to leave his safe
green field, to go to a forest where, in the past,
he had personally met – in this order:

a leopard

a dragon (just one but it had two heads)

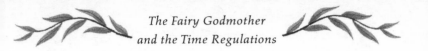

wolves (a family)

brigands (very bad brigands).

And he was now looking for bears.

Not even Florizella felt very brave as they went deeper and deeper into the wood, and the branches overhead blotted out the light. It was called the Purple Forest because from a distance, from her bedroom window in the castle, the endless trees had a purple haze in the evening light. Florizella thought that the Purple Forest was at it's best when seen from a distance. Now that she was actually inside the forest at dusk it was not purple; it was shadowy and dark. And the trees creaked as if they were about to fall on her. And the dried leaves on the path rustled as if something was following

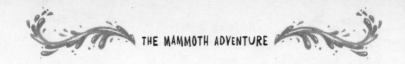

her. And the wind sighed in the branches of the trees as if it was saying *whooo-whooo* rather like a . . .

Florizella stopped herself thinking what might go *whooo-whooo* in a dark, thickly wooded forest, and instead concentrated on following the path as Jellybean went slower and slower, with his head drooping lower and lower, and Florizella had to whistle a happy little tune to keep her spirits up.

Maybe it was because she wasn't very good at whistling; maybe it was because she did not know a happy little tune right at that moment, but her spirits sank lower and lower. Her courage ebbed away, bit by bit, as they went deeper and deeper into the forest. She was very relieved to arrive at the little clearing with the stream and the cave where they had left Bear, hoping that he would love his new life in the wild, but secretly fearing that he might not.

And there was the picnic hamper! Perhaps everything was fine. The lid was shut, so maybe he had eaten the sandwiches and then shut the lid with the litter inside, as any tidy, sensible bear would do.

Florizella jumped down from Jellybean and tied the pony to a tree. She looked around to see if Bear was anywhere near. Jellybean looked around too, hoping very much to see nothing – no bear and definitely not a dragon. Florizella opened the lid of the basket, expecting to see a couple of wrappers and perhaps the well-sucked stick of a lollipop . . .

But *there* was the entire picnic – untouched!

This was very bad indeed.

And, on the top, a note written with a clumsy red crayon in very bad writing . . . A rather terrible note to read, it said:

We hAve KidhAppeD the BeAR
AhD we wiLL ohLy RetuRh him
FOR A huGe RAhsOm.
BRihG £500 heRe At six O'CLOCK.
OR ThAt BeAR Is TOASt.
Five-FAthOm FRieDA

Florizella sat down on the grass with a bump, as if her legs had given way beneath her. 'Oh no!' she said. 'Oh no! This has all gone Terribly Wrong.'

It didn't take Florizella more than a few moments to realise that she had to get help if she was going to rescue Bear from unknown numbers of pirates, headed by Five-Fathom Frieda, arriving at six o'clock. It didn't take Florizella very long to realise that she had only a couple of hours of daylight left to get help, as it was just after lunch when she had left the palace.

She reached into her rucksack and pulled out a messenger bird called Swithin. He was a little green parrot, new to the work and very eager.

'Swithin,' said Florizella, 'you're to find Prince Courier and then Prince Bennett and give them this message.'

Swithin put up his little green crest and said, '*Cark!*'

Florizella looked at him a little doubtfully. 'I'll take that as a yes,' she said. 'Now listen – this is very important. Here is the message: *No picnic eaten. Not even jelly. Not fishpaste. Pirates have Bear. Come at once. Jump to it for his sake.* Can you remember that?'

'*Cark!*' said Swithin.

'Good,' said Florizella. 'Repeat it back to me.'

'*No picnic eaten,*' began the parrot. It even sounded like it was Florizella speaking. Swithin copied her voice as well as memorising the words. '*Not even jelly. Not fishpaste. Pirates have bear. Come at once. Jump to it for his sake.*'

'That's perfect,' said Florizella, more surprised than she would like to admit. 'Now go to Prince

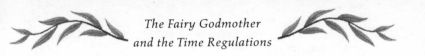

Courier and tell him all that. I'll wait here.'

Swithin nodded, spread his little green wings, took a leap into the air and shot upwards. He circled once overhead as if to note exactly where Florizella was, and then confidently headed north for Prince Bennett's castle in the Land of Deep Lakes.

'No!' Florizella yelled from the ground below. 'I said go to Courier first! Not Bennett!'

But Swithin was gone.

CHAPTER THREE

*Of which there is almost
nothing to say but Courier's
favourite new word: alasss*

*B*ennett was training his lizard. He
had intended to take up the more
interesting and fashionable hobby of dragon
taming but, when he told his father, the king
had said, 'Bennett – listen to me, Son. Start
with a lizard. They're more intelligent and if it
goes wrong you won't have been eaten by your
own pet.'

'But lizards can't fly!' Bennett objected.

'They can't burn down the castle, either,' his father said. 'Start with a lizard, Bennett, and, when you can get it to sit, lie down and walk to heel, I'll see about finding you a dragon.'

'I never get anything,' Bennett said most untruthfully.

'I know,' his father said, pretending to agree with him. 'You are most cruelly treated.'

Bennett didn't find this at all funny. 'You don't even mean that,' he complained.

'I don't!' said his father cheerfully. 'Seems to me that you and Florizella get everything you want. How her parents put up with a Sea Serpent in the moat is beyond me! You needn't think you're going to have one here.'

'But I don't want one!' Bennett protested. 'I just want a really small dragon.'

'Lizard,' his father said. 'It's almost the same thing.'

Bennett knew there was no point in arguing, so he took the train to the Bay of Reptiles, lassoed a medium-size lizard – one about the size of a large dog – and started to train it.

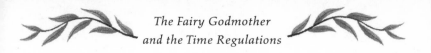

He had just got it to sit and was rewarding it with a mouthful of dried insects when a green parrot flew in the open window and perched on the curtain rail.

'Message?' Bennett asked.

'*Cark.*'

'You're Swithin, aren't you?'

'*Cark.*'

'Prince Courier's messenger parrot?'

'*Cark.*'

'I thought you flew between Princess Florizella and Prince Courier?'

'*Cark.*'

'It's not much use being a messenger parrot that doesn't speak,' Bennett said severely. 'Get on with it then.'

Swithin opened his beak and had a terrible

moment. His little mind had gone completely blank. He looked at Bennett in surprise. '*Cark?*' he said.

'Yes, you said,' Bennett pointed out a little impatiently. 'But what's the message?'

Dimly, the words came back to Swithin. *No picnic eaten*, he thought. '*No panic, Beaton,*' he said. He looked at Prince Bennett's puzzled face and thought he had got the name wrong. '*No panic, Bennett,*' he said reassuringly. What came next? Was it something that sounded like '*Not even jelly*'?

'*Naughty and smelly,*' it told him.

'What?'

'*Fishface,*' he went on. '*Pirates are bare.*'

'What did you say?' Bennett demanded.

In his anxiety, the little parrot garbled the

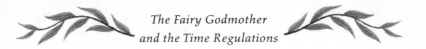

rest of the message.

'*Complete dunce. Jump in the lake.*'

'Did you just tell me to jump in the lake?' Bennett demanded.

'*Cark,*' said Swithin with quiet pride. He remembered, a little late, that he was supposed to go to Courier first and without another word, spread his little green wings and flew out of the window.

'You come back here!' Bennett shouted as Swithin rose in the sky.

'*Fishface!*' Bennett heard him say as he headed off to find Courier. '*Jump in the lake.*'

Bennett saddled up his horse to rode over to Florizella's castle, his face burning red with rage at the insults from Swithin the green parrot. But, as he entered the Land of the Seven

Kingdoms, he saw Prince Courier, Florizella's brother, riding to meet him on his pony.

'I thought I'd come and find you,' Courier said. 'I've just had a messenger parrot tell me not to panic, but that you are naughty and smelly.'

Bennett ground his teeth. 'Told me to jump in the lake. If I catch him, I'll wring his neck.'

'No, that bit wasn't jump in the lake. I think it was supposed to be "for his sake",' Courier explained. 'But I don't know whose sake. It was very muddled. I asked him to repeat the message and he called me a dunce.'

'But why was Florizella sending a messenger parrot anyway?'

'Oh . . .' said Courier. 'That's right! That was why I was coming to find you.'

'Where is she?'

Courier suddenly remembered the important bit. Then he remembered it was hugely important, and he had allowed himself to be distracted again. 'Oh yes! Sorry! My mistake. I should have said at once. She's gone deep into the Purple Forest on her pony, to look for Bear. I think she might be in danger. That's probably why she sent a messenger parrot. She said she would send word if she needed us. Me and Mammoth and Sea Serpent are backup.'

'You think Florizella might have fallen in a trap or been eaten and you forget to tell me?' Bennett demanded. 'When Florizella is in danger?'

'Yes,' Courier admitted. 'Sorry about that.

I should have come quicker and told you at once. So . . . right . . . she's disappeared into the Purple Forest and sent a message, so she probably needs help. We should probably have gone to help her as soon as the parrot arrived. Alasss.'

Bennett scowled at Florizella's irritating little brother. 'What?'

'Alasss,' Courier repeated.

'Luckily for you,' Bennett said heavily, 'Florizella is not the sort of girl who needs rescuing. And, luckily for me, she doesn't mind me joining in – even in an emergency. Luckily for you, she said you were to be backup. That's the only reason I'm allowing you to come with me. So, come on.'

The two of them urged their ponies into a

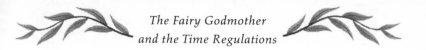

canter and followed the winding path deep into the forest.

While this unreliable rescue party was finally setting out, Florizella was wondering how she was going to defeat Five-Fathom Frieda and her dastardly crew of pirates to rescue Bear. They were a long way from the sea for a pirate band, so Florizella guessed that they had most likely set up an evil pirate camp inland, probably nearby, deep in the Purple Forest.

First, Florizella thought they might have left marks on the muddy ground and she would be able to track them. But Florizella and Courier had come and gone, and then Florizella had arrived again, and, there were many hoofprints in the mud, going in all directions. Jellybean helpfully matched his hoof to one print, as if to show that there was no way of tracking the pirates and it would be better by far for both him and Florizella to go home, and for him, in particular, to go back to his nice safe stable.

But all she said was, 'Yes, I know. They're your hoofprints. The pirates probably came on foot. And Bear doesn't leave prints at all because he has pads on his paws.'

Jellybean sighed and realised that he was not going back to the stable any time soon, but he was too loyal a horse to slip away and go home alone. He gave her a rather regretful look. If he had been Courier, he would have said, 'Alasss.'

'I just wish I knew where Bear was,' Florizella

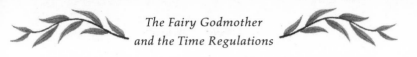

said longingly. 'I wish with all my heart that I knew where they'd taken him.'

To her surprise, there was an explosion above her head, and a small fairy fell out of the overhanging branches of a nearby tree.

CHAPTER FOUR

*In which we meet
an overworked
fairy godmother*

ellybean startled back in shock as the
fairy tumbled head over heels into a
bush. She pulled herself out of the branches
and brushed off fairy dust, which sparkled as
it fell to the ground. A couple of twigs clung
to her hair. She straightened her wand, which
had been bent in the fall.

She was a very small fairy, less than half
Florizella's height. She could have been any

age – up to about 400 years. She wore a fairy gown in yellow, like a party dress, but it was so old that it was ragged at the hem held together with pins. Around her neck she had a number of scarves in silver and gold that floated around, getting wrapped up in the large wings folded down her back. Her hair was pink, her expression completely baffled.

'Oh gracious, not again!' she exclaimed, catching a trailing scarf that had wrapped itself round her waist. 'And which one are you?' she asked Florizella. 'I suppose it was you who has to have a wish granted? All in a moment and never a please or a thank you?'

Jellybean looked hopeful for a moment – he had been wishing to go home for some time. Indeed, he had wished that they had never come. He was perfectly prepared to say "please" or "thank you". But the fairy was not speaking to him. She glowered up at Florizella. 'Which one are you?' she repeated irritably. 'For heaven's sake!' She grabbed another scarf that had twisted round her feet.

'Which one?'

'Yes, which one! Which one! Which one! You just pulled me through a hedge backwards without the least notice, suddenly throwing a true wish a "wish with all your heart!" into the air, so I can't ignore it! I suppose that you're one of mine, though I have so many I can hardly be expected to tell one from t'other. And indeed I don't. I can't! Don't even want to!'

'You came because I wished?' Florizella asked, trying to drag some sense out of the squeaks of outrage.

'I had to! If you're one of my godchildren! I don't get any choice do I? So which one are you? You can't be Sophronia because she never wishes for anything seriously. She just makes a list of sweets and presents, but she never has a wish with all her heart. Treats me like some sort of delivery service. I told her – I'm a fairy godmother not a postie.'

'I'm not Sophronia,' Florizella began. 'I'm . . .'

'And you can't be Jezackerly because I saw her last week when she wished for peace for all the world.' The fairy tutted. 'She only does it to look good in her wishing class. As though I could deliver world peace in Flatland just because she wished for it! Do you have any idea how many people there are in Flatland? And how quarrelsome they are? And how little attention they pay to fairies?'

'I'm not Jezackerly,' Florizella said humbly.

'You can't be Petersweet because he's another fanciful wisher – raindrops on roses, whiskers on kittens. Not even original. I mean, I *can* do things like that – anyone competent can – but what's the point of them? It's nothing but conjuring tricks – like rabbits out of a hat. And what's the use of having a rabbit in your top hat? They always poo in the hat, you know. So, days after you've forgotten your very clever conjuring trick, long after your audience has gone away, you put on your coat, you pop your top hat on your head, and there you are with a load of rabbit poo in your hair. Not so very clever then, are you?'

'I suppose not,' Florizella said, feeling more and more confused. 'My name is Florizella. I'm the princess of the Seven Kingdoms.'

The fairy hunted through her pockets and put on a pair of glasses. She peered at her.

'You're Florizella?' she confirmed.

'Yes.'

'Quite sure?'

'Yes,' Florizella said. 'Certain.'

'I've not seen you before,' the fairy said severely as if this was Florizella's fault.

'No, I don't think so,' Florizella admitted. 'I'm delighted to meet you, of course, and excuse me, but who are you?'

'I am your fairy godmother!' the fairy announced grandly, twisting a gauzy scarf round her neck. 'Fairy Fata your fairy godmother. And I have come to grant your wish.'

'Right,' Florizella said, a bit surprised. 'I didn't know I had a fairy godmother, you see. No one ever mentioned you to me.'

'Never mentioned your fairy godmother?

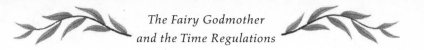
Never mentioned me?'

Florizella shook her head.

'Heavens, how rude! What were your parents thinking of? They never even mentioned me?'

'I am sorry. I'm sure there has been some misunderstanding,' Florizella said on her best royal behaviour. 'Have you come far?'

'Of course I've come far, you silly girl!' Fairy Fata exclaimed irritably, pulling the rest of the twigs out of her pink hair. 'All the way from Fairyland, tumbling through space and time and possibly other dimensions to arrive – *pouf!* – here! At the whim of a god-daughter who has never even heard of me, who has some nonsensical wish about a bear!'

'That was me.' Florizella agreed to the only thing she could understand. 'I didn't know I was calling you. I was just wishing that I knew where Bear was. He's been kidnapped, you see. Captured by pirates. And, since it was me who left him in the forest, I have to rescue him.'

'Well, at least you're not wishing for world peace,' Fairy Fata said begrudgingly. 'I can't stand it when they do that. Better to get on and work for it than stand about wishing, I tell them. But a bear? I should be able to get you a bear.' She raised her wand. 'Polar bear?' she asked. 'Panda? Dancing? Any special features?'

'Stop!' Florizella shrieked. 'Not any sort of bear! The very last thing I want is another bear. I've got one more than my father wants already! I want a particular bear, a very special bear. A spectacled bear. I call him Bear.'

'Imaginative,' said the fairy nastily. 'Not

even a fairytale christening.'

'He was born in a show and doesn't know how to live in the wild,' Florizella went on, too worried to notice her godmother's lack of enthusiasm. 'And now Five-Fathom Frieda and her pirate band have captured him and I just wish I could get him back.'

'Now here's a difficulty,' Fairy Fata said, lowering her wand. 'Did you say Five-Fathom Frieda?'

'Yes,' said Florizella. 'So, could you just wish her back on her ship at sea, and bring Bear back here? That's all my wishes. And I promise not to wish for anything else for months. For ever if you like.'

'That's not the problem,' the fairy godmother told her. 'The problem is that Five-Fathom Frieda is one of mine too.'

'One of your what?'

'One of my godchildren. One of my many hundreds and hundreds of godchildren! And she woke this morning and wished for everything that Florizella had today and so – whoosh! – I took your bear and your picnic, both together. Really fast. Two in one go. Before I'd even had breakfast.'

'It was you who took my bear?' Florizella said accusingly.

'And the picnic,' the fairy nodded.

'She didn't even come herself to steal my things?'

'Why would she make any effort when she just has to wish?'

'But the picnic's here!' Florizella exclaimed.

'She said it was yucky.'

'Yucky!' Florizella was quite distracted by

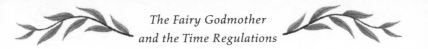

her irritation about this. 'How rude!'

'So I brought it back. She wished for the ransom note too.'

'She insulted my picnic and didn't even write her own ransom note?'

'No. It's me who has to do all the work for her, all the work for all of you!'

'How many godchildren have you got, exactly?' Florizella was quite horrified at the thought of so many people – including really bad ones like Five-Fathom Frieda – being able to wish for anything they wanted. Why wouldn't Frieda wish for endless treasure? And how many other people could ask for anything they wanted?

'Don't know. Definitely hundreds,' Fairy Fata said gloomily. 'Maybe thousands. I'm not allowed to refuse an invitation to a christening, you see. And everyone has to invite all the fairies for fear of any one of us staying away and casting a curse. So everyone invites all of us, and all of us have to go.'

'Do you have to grant every wish?' Florizella was appalled. 'Even if people wish for bad things?'

'There are regulations,' the fairy godmother admitted. 'There are very strict regulations.'

'There should be a regulation to stop someone wishing for someone else's bear!' Florizella said irritably.

'You shouldn't own a bear at all!' the fairy replied. 'He should be free.'

'I was trying to set him free when you kidnapped him!' Florizella exclaimed. 'But why would Frieda want a picnic and a bear? She's a pirate! Why would she need such things?'

'Because they're yours,' Fairy Fata said. 'She wants whatever you've got. Ever since she first saw you on the Queasy Quays that day. She liked the look of your brother and your friend and your parents. She wants them too. She wants your wolf.'

'Dog,' Florizella corrected.

'Whatever. She wants a pony like yours. She'll probably wish for it in a moment. And *pouf!* It'll be gone. She's just starting with your bear. Warming up, you might say, for her Big List.'

'She wants my life?' Florizella asked, quite horrified.

'One bit at a time,' the fairy confirmed. 'And if she wishes for it – I have to give it to her.'

'Can't I get everything back again by wishing?'

'Yes,' the fairy agreed reluctantly. 'But then she can get them back again from you. And I have to deliver them. And that can go on – to you – to her – to you – to her – forward and back till I die of exhaustion, carrying ponies and brothers and bears through space and time for two thoroughly spoiled godchildren.'

'I'm not spoiled,' Florizella pointed out. 'I didn't even know I had a fairy godmother until you took my bear and picnic and gave them to someone else. That's not exactly spoiling.'

'No,' Fairy Fata agreed reluctantly. 'I suppose it isn't. But it's still hard work for me.'

'Can you go to Five-Fathom Frieda and tell her that she can't have my things, and that she's to stop wishing for them?' Florizella asked.

The fairy shook her head. 'It's my job to

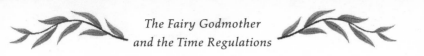
grant wishes, not judge them,' she said. 'I have to fulfil the wish. However stupid. Unless it's against regulations.'

She put her head on one side as if she was listening to a faraway shout and exclaimed: 'Bother! There she goes again!'

'Is it Frieda? What does she want now?' Florizella demanded with sudden dread. She tightened her grip on the reins and put her arms round her pony's warm neck. 'Not my Jellybean?'

Fairy Fata did not even trouble herself to reply. There was a whirl of wind, like a very small, very strong tornado, and the fairy rose off the ground, her scarves madly spinning round her. With a sudden *POP* - she was gone.

CHAPTER FIVE

This is just like a proper fairy tale with a fairy godmother and everything!

ennett and Courier were not far from the clearing where Florizella had left Bear and the picnic.

'You're sure it was here?' Bennett asked.

'Positive,' Courier replied. 'Look – hoofprints on the ground.'

'They could be anybody's,' Bennett said.

'I know they're mine.' Courier jumped down from his pony and pointed to the size of the

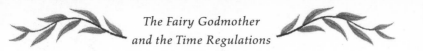

hoofprint. 'See? I was here before, and look – I went home that way.'

'That's a great relief,' Bennett said sarcastically. 'I couldn't be happier to have proof that you went safely home. But it's Florizella we're worried about – and when you trit-trotted home, she went out again. And, since you didn't raise the alarm, we didn't get here in time, and now we don't know where she's gone.'

'Now, if we had a map that showed where we are and where she is . . .' Courier started to say, when they heard a strange *whoosh* and a *POP* behind him. When Bennett looked, Courier had completely disappeared. All that was left was a rather surprised pony with trailing reins, and nothing at all at the other end of them.

'Courier?' Bennett asked, 'Courier, if you're

messing about hiding, then come out. We've got to back-up Florizella, remember? We're a rescue party! You can't just vanish when we're on an adventure.'

There was no sound at all. Just the tiniest tinkle of falling fairy dust.

'Courier?' Bennett said a little more anxiously. 'Courier!'

He caught the reins of Courier's pony, holding his own horse tightly, and he bellowed at the top of his voice: 'COURIER! COURIER!'

'No need to shout,' Florizella remarked, suddenly appearing. Jellybean, looking very dejected, was walking along behind her. 'Gosh! Has he gone too?'

Bennett gaped at her. 'Vanished into thin air. Are you OK?'

'Yes, I'm fine,' Florizella said sounding not-fine-at-all. 'Just that everything I own and love is being stolen from me, one thing at a time, by Five-Fathom Frieda. She wishes that she had them, and my fairy godmother – my own fairy godmother! – delivers them to her.'

Bennett looked at her with his mouth agape. But he went at once to the most unlikely part of the whole incredible story. 'Five-Fathom Frieda wants Courier? She can't do.'

Glumly, Florizella nodded. Jellybean was glum too.

'But why? She can't possibly have wished for Courier. That must be a mistake. Has she ever spent any time with him?'

'No, but she saw him standing on the whale, remember? When he thought it was an island?

Just think how useful it would be to a pirate captain to have someone who could find islands. She probably didn't know that not only did he *not* find an island, he is dangerously incapable of recognising a whale.'

'She'll send him back,' Bennett said with certainty. 'Nobody would keep Courier for more than half a day. He'll invent something for her and it will be completely useless.'

'We can't risk it,' Florizella said. 'Mummy Queen and Daddy King are sure to ask where he is at teatime. And anyway – what about Bear – Frieda's taken him too – and I have to find Bear.'

'Can we follow Courier?' Bennett asked. 'Can you wish us there?'

Florizella looked doubtful. 'If we just appear by magic, then Five-Fathom Frieda could just wish us away again. What I really want to do, is sneak up on Five-Fathom Frieda, rescue Bear and Courier without her knowing, and then make her promise to go back to proper piracy and stop wishing for my things,' Florizella said. 'And then I want to get hold of the fairy godmother and make her stop.'

'Stop her granting wishes?'

'There are rules about what can be granted, she told me. They should certainly not allow stealing!'

Bennett was silent for a moment, then he said: 'I might have a Brilliant Plan.'

'Oh yes?' Florizella trusted Bennett – often he actually did have a Brilliant Plan.

'Why don't you wish that you knew where Five-Fathom Frieda was hiding Bear and Courier?

And we could sneak up on them, rescue Bear and Courier, capture her and force her to stop.'

'Now that *is* a Brilliant Plan,' Florizella agreed. She spread her hands wide, closed her eyes and said: 'I wish I knew where Five-Fathom Frieda was keeping Courier and Bear.'

There was a rather irritable clang – not a pleasant fairy tinkle at all – and Florizella clapped her hand to her forehead as if someone had bashed her in the face with a frying pan. 'Got it!' she said. 'Though that was rather hard.'

'For heaven's sake!' came an irritable squeak from the blue sky. 'You wished hard.'

'Where are they?' Bennett asked, watching all this with interest.

'On Frieda's pirate ship, by the Queasy Quays,' Florizella said. 'We hardly needed a wish for

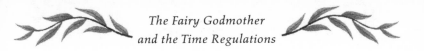

that actually — we could have figured it out for ourselves.'

'Exactly!' said the distant voice. 'Spoiled and now lazy.'

Bennett inched over to Florizella. 'She's not very nice, is she?' he whispered. 'I mean, if she's the good fairy godmother, and she slaps you in the face with your wish and calls you spoiled and lazy, what do you think the wicked one is like?'

Florizella widened her eyes. 'Please tell me I haven't got a wicked fairy godmother as well as this one!'

Bennett shrugged. 'I don't know,' he said. 'But I didn't know until now that you'd got a good fairy godmother. And I've never seen any of mine. How does anyone know if they've got them or not?'

Florizella looked quite horrified. 'There could be dozens of them,' she said. 'All waiting to join in some ridiculous fairy tale when I get put to sleep and you have to cut your way through the forest. Or I get imprisoned in an impossibly tall tower and you climb up. Or I get put in a glass coffin and you kiss me awake! Whatever the story - the princess is always stuck somewhere, waiting, and the princes get all the adventures.'

Bennett nodded. 'I can see it's unfair,' he said.

'It's completely ridiculous,' Florizella declared. 'And as soon as we've got Bear back, and Courier, I'm going to abolish fairy godmothers!'

CHAPTER SIX

*In which Bennett
meets a fan*

Florizella and Bennett left the three horses in the field at the Purple Forest station, and boarded the train for the seaside. The two royals glanced up at the sky and saw that, high above them, a Good Manner Eagle was circling. At once, they were on their very best behaviour.

'After you,' Prince Bennett said, holding the train door open for Florizella.

'No – after you,' Florizella replied, letting him go first.

'Thank you so much,' Bennett said, getting into the carriage and then putting out a hand to pull Florizella in after him.

'Thank *you*,' she said politely as she shut the door and the train drew out of the station.

The guard, a wallaby with his ticket machine in her pouch, came up to check their tickets. 'The service has been delayed by Unforeseen Circumstances,' she said. 'The engine has broken down and been replaced with Temporary Support.'

'What support?' Florizella asked.

'The Mammoth is pushing

the train,' the guard explained.

'My Mammoth?' Florizella asked.

The wallaby guard raised her eyebrows. 'He's a free Mammoth,' she pointed out. 'You don't own him, Your Royal Highness.'

'No, of course I don't,' Florizella corrected herself. 'This isn't old Fairytale Land, when everything belonged to the king. I don't own anyone. I meant the Mammoth I know. My friend the Mammoth.'

'That one,' the wallaby agreed. 'That's the one. The only one in Fairytale Land actually.'

There was a little bump in the carriage as the Mammoth put his big forehead to the back of the train and started to push. Florizella and Bennett leaned out of the window and saw his large fluffy ginger shoulder and the side of his ear. They heard him humming as he pushed the train along.

'He loves the work,' said the wallaby guard. 'He's very reliable.'

Florizella and Bennett sat down again and watched out of the window as the train stopped at the stations of Rock Pools and Sandy Bay before it arrived at the final destination of the Queasy Quays.

'So, how do we sneak up?' Florizella asked.

'We have to see how the enemy is placed,' Bennett said. 'We go under cover.'

The two royal children got themselves in the middle of the queue of passengers getting off the train and, by ducking down behind a milkmaid with her cow, managed to slip along the platform unseen.

'Hide and Seek?" the Mammoth said hopefully, spotting them as he was getting ready to push the train up to top of the Unscalable Cliffs to the train turntable.

'No,' Bennett told him. 'A Brilliant Plan.'

'Shall I come too?' the Mammoth asked eagerly. 'I could be bwilliant.' He looked down his trunk. 'I am quite bwave, you know.'

'I know,' Florizella told him. 'But this is between me and the pirate. Would you turn the train around so that it faces back home again, and be our getaway driver?'

'Oh yes!' the Mammoth agreed quickly. 'I'll do that! I'll be weady.'

'You're my back-up,' Florizella smiled at him.

'And Sea Serpent is in the bay,' he told her. 'It is back-up too.'

The two royals mingled with the crowd and made their way down to the Queasy Quays without being spotted by any of the crew of the pirate ship *Boney*. The ship, a brigantine, was in a terribly untidy state. Knots of rope were tangled up on deck and the sails were flapping - half up and half down. Someone had dumped the anchor on the quay, and the ropes tying the ship to the shore were twisted and knitted together as if they would never be untied again. Five-Fathom Frieda herself was seated amidships watching the loading of cargo – barrels and barrels of food and strong drink. Every now and then, she shouted: 'More grog!'

Florizella and Bennett, hiding behind some crates could see Bear, patiently scrubbing the wooden floor, a bucket and mop beside him, and – leaning on another mop, talking and talking to Frieda, but actually doing no actual work at all – there was Courier.

Bennett and Florizella crept along the quayside, ducking behind boxes and suitcases until they were close enough to hear Courier explaining to Five-Fathom Frieda: 'You speak into one end, wherever you are, and at the other end, the person hears you.'

'He's still going on about a telephone?' Florizella whispered to Bennett.

'Unstoppably.'

'And what do they say back?' Frieda asked.

Courier hesitated. 'They say whatever they want.'

'I'm not having that,' the pirate chief

objected. 'I'm not having people say whatever they want to me.'

'It's a device for listening,' Courier tried to explain. 'Over huge distances.'

'I don't want to listen to anybody. Near or far.'

'You could use it to tell people things?' Courier suggested.

'I can shout,' Frieda pointed out. 'I can bellow.'

'Over very long distances?'

'I am extremely loud,' she said with pride.

'But what about their reply?'

'I don't care about their reply.'

Florizella and Bennett could see that Courier was – for once in his life – completely stumped.

'I'm a pirate,' Frieda explained to him. 'I'm

not interested in conversation. I hunt for treasure and steal it. I give orders. I don't talk to people – I shout at them.'

'But why?' Courier asked her. 'Why go to all the trouble of hunting and stealing if you can just wish for things? Like the way you got me. And Bear. If you think about it, you will see that pirating is a complete waste of your time.'

Frieda's big moon face turned to him in surprise. 'A waste of my time?' she asked. 'It's all I know how to do! Being a pirate is all I've ever done.'

'Yes, but that was before you discovered your fairy godmother,' Courier said. 'Now you know that you have a godmother, you don't have to go looking for treasure – you can just wish for it.'

'I can?'

'Of course. No need to put to sea, no need to sail the Spanish Main or anybody's main anything. No need to shout orders to anyone but your fairy godmother. Just tell her what you want!'

'I want Princess Florizella's things,' Frieda said enviously. 'All of them.'

'Well, obviously you can just get them! And really there's no point wishing for them one at a time. Why not make a complete list and wish for them all at once?'

'Oh, thanks very much, Courier,' Florizella muttered crossly into Bennett's ear.

'Could I have her castle? And everything in it?' Frieda asked eagerly.

Courier hesitated. 'Not here,' he said. 'There's the gardens and the gates and the moat. It wouldn't fit on the Quays. Certainly not on the good ship *Boney*.'

'*Bonny*,' Frieda said. 'My ship is the *Bonny*.'

Courier was about to tell her that the name written on the side of the ship, spelled *Boney*, but then he thought she probably didn't like contradictions any more than conversation, so he said nothing.

'I want her castle,' Frieda said stubbornly. 'Do I have to shout at you?'

'What you want,' Courier said persuasively. 'What you really want is to be royal isn't it? Like us? And live in the castle with all of us — her family? Then you can have all of her things whenever you want them.'

Florizella leaned towards Bennett and said: 'I can't believe this! My own brother! Isn't this treason? Giving my life away?'

'I'm hoping he has a Plan,' Bennett whispered back. 'Even if it's not Brilliant.'

'I don't want her at the castle,' Frieda said meanly. 'I want her gone. I don't want her riding her pony – my pony!'

'Your ponny,' Courier said, smiling to himself.

'What?'

'Nothing. I quite understand about you wanting everything. Even the pony.' Courier put his mop to one side and made himself a comfortable seat on an upturned bucket. 'What you really want is to BE her. Isn't it?'

Frieda clasped her big hands together. 'Yes!' she breathed. 'I want to be a princess and wear beautiful dresses, and go to balls, and have a

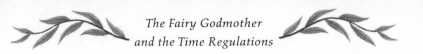

chest full of the crown jewels that I haven't stolen from anyone because they're all mine. And I want you to be my little brother, and Prince Bennett—'

She broke off, a rosy flush spreading across her face, and drew a line on the deck with the big toe of her enormous sea boot. 'I want Prince Bennett as my husband. My own Prince Charming. I think I'll marry him,' she said.

CHAPTER SEVEN

*Five-Fathom Frieda
discovers the Princess Rules*

lorizella clamped her hand over
Bennett's mouth to stifle his shriek
of protest. 'Shh,' she whispered fiercely to
him. 'If she wishes it out loud, and her fairy
godmother hears, then it's your wedding day
and I'm bridesmaid.'

Bennett's dark eyes boggled above Florizella's
hand.

'You'll be quiet?' she demanded.

Bennett nodded. Carefully, Florizella released him.

'She must be stopped!' Bennett hissed. 'At once! This has gone too far!'

'It's worse for me than for you,' Florizella pointed out. 'If she gets her way, you're Mr Five-Fathom Frieda, for happily ever after, but what happens to me? She wants me gone.'

'We'd better capture her at once,' Bennett said. 'Before she starts wishing for anything. Before that idiot Courier tells her to wish for me!'

'But how?'

'Rush and grab?' Bennett suggested. 'If only I'd brought my sword.'

'I've got a dagger in my boot,' Florizella said in a modest sort of voice.

'Course you have,' Bennett said enviously. 'Always! But that's not enough. They've got a crew of twenty, a weapons' room, a gunpowder room and cutlasses.'

'We've got Courier on board,' Florizella pointed out.

'I don't know if that is an advantage or not,' Bennett said gloomily. 'Just listen to him now . . .'

Courier and Frieda had strolled together to the far side of the ship, chatting happily. They were practically arm in arm: the best of friends. Bennett and Florizella crept up the gangplank and ducked down behind a couple of barrels in the middle of the deck. Bear widened his eyes as he saw them hiding, but he went on mopping slowly, saying nothing. All the other

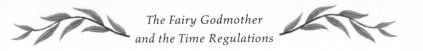

pirates had left the ship as soon as Five-Fathom Frieda had stopped watching them. They were sitting on the quayside, having a rest, gloomily comparing the blisters on their hands from scrubbing the deck.

On board, Courier was still advising Frieda. 'There's just one hitch: Bennett can't marry anyone who isn't a princess.'

'He can't?'

'No, so the first thing to do would be to wish yourself royal – and then the rest will just simply follow. The crown jewels, the castle and the handsome prince.'

'I'll do that then,' Frieda decided and, before Bennett and Florizella could spring forward and grab her, she closed her eyes and said: 'I wish, I wish, I wish I was a royal princess.'

There was a *whoosh* and a *POP!* and then *BANG!* There was Five-Fathom Frieda, just the same as ever in her big sea boots with a cutlass in her belt, but crammed on top of her huge pirate hat was a sparkling tiara, and rolling out across the deck under her muddy boots was a bright red carpet.

'Blimey,' said Courier. 'Your fairy godmother is quick.'

'Exhausted!' came a voice from somewhere up in the rigging. 'Worn to a shred! At the end of my tether! And never a word of thanks.'

'I wish I had a mirror,' Frieda remarked touching her crown.

There was an almighty crash and a huge gold-framed mirror fell down from the crow's nest at the top of the mast and splintered into a thousand sharp pieces on the deck.

'Slipped!' came the voice from the rigging. 'Not surprising really. I'm beside myself.'

'I wish I had a mirror that I could see myself in!' Frieda bellowed upwards, clearly irritated at not getting her own way. 'Now!'

BANG! again! And now there was a long

pier glass standing unbroken on the deck before the pirate captain. She gave a little gasp at her reflection, and turned one way and then the other, admiring herself from the topmost sparkling stone in her tiara to the crimson carpet under her boots.

'Your Royal Highness.' Courier bowed, and she beamed at him. 'But now that you're royal there are a few things you have to do,' he said.

'No I don't! I don't have to do anything,' Princess Frieda snapped. 'I always do only what I want.'

Overhead, in the sky, there was a small dot, circling.

'We could rush her now,' Bennett whispered. 'While she's distracted by the tiara and the red carpet.'

'Hang on a minute,' Florizella said. She pointed upwards where the dot had come a little lower, almost as if an eagle was looking down and listening. 'Hang on a minute, Bennett. I know it's surprising, but it may be that Courier has, right now, a Brilliant Plan.'

'But you have to have good manners if you're royal,' Courier said gently. 'You have to say "please" and "thank you", and you can never take anything that isn't yours. You have to be kind, think about others, step back and ask people if they'd like to go first, ask them if they've come far . . . that sort of thing. There are Princess Rules and you have to obey them.'

'I'm not doing any of that,' Princess Five-Fathom Frieda declared roundly. 'I'm not wasting my time on any of that stupid stuff.'

'You have to always be on time, never keep anyone waiting,' Courier said as if speaking his thoughts aloud, one eye on the sky where the dot was now clearly one, two and three large birds, circling round and round. 'Speaking nicely, not shouting, never grabbing.'

The new royal princess Five-Fathom Frieda was bored of Courier. She shot out one great hand, grabbed him by the throat and yelled in his face. 'Who d'you think you are? You don't tell me what to do! Nobody tells me what to do! I'll shout, and grab, and be late, and steal all I want. More! Much more now that I'm royal! Now I'm royal, I own everything, don't I? It's all mine!'

There was a screaming noise of air rushing through six feathered wings and three Good

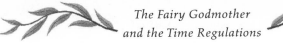

Manner Eagles came roaring down to the deck. Two of them grabbed Princess Five-Fathom Frieda by each arm, and the third got her by the scruff of her coat collar. They lifted her, their huge wings beating a powerful wind that filled the sails and made the ship shudder at her mooring. Frieda rose off the deck, her feet kicking in mid-air and gold doubloons falling out of her bulging pockets.

'Oh! No, no, no, no, no, no, no, no, no, no!' the first Good Manner Eagle said reproachfully. 'Indeed no!'

Politeness is a princess's greatest gift!

They recited. Flapping their wings, they gave Frieda a little shake that rippled through her whole body and caused a cascade of stolen treasure to tumble down to the deck below from hiding places in her jacket, trousers and hat. Florizella saw a brooch her mother had lost a year ago, and Bennett recognised some silver knives and forks that carried his royal crest.

'Put me down!' bellowed Five-Fathom Frieda at the Good Manner Eagles. Everyone on the quayside, everyone in the little seaside town beside it turned and looked skywards to see the source of the terrific noise. The lighthouse keeper started to climb the stairs up to her light to switch it on, thinking she had heard the foghorn.

In silent reply, the eagles all rose together and hovered over the sea, Princess Frieda dangled helplessly below them.

'You stupid eagles! Put me down!' she ordered them. 'Or I'll turn you to stone with one wish!'

'If we turned to stone you would plunge, from quite a great height, into the sea,' one Good Manner Eagle pointed out. 'With regrettable damage to yourself, and certain loss of any remaining stolen treasure that you have concealed about your person.'

Frieda's legs in the big boots pedalled in space like a champion cyclist. 'I'll pluck you – stupid bird!' she shouted.

'Very rude!' the third eagle observed. 'And an empty threat, since you cannot reach us. Pray observe that it is you dangling at a dangerous height over the sea, and it is us who are holding you up.'

'When I get down, I'll shoot you!' Frieda modified her threat. 'With my blunderbuss.'

'You had much better agree not to be royal any more, and make that your last and final wish,' the first Good Manner Eagle told her severely. 'You would find that being royal does not suit someone of your adventurous temperament. You would find that being royal is tedious for someone as selfish as you. You had much better go back to being a pirate where you can be as rude as you like. Indeed, it is expected of you.'

Frieda, too angry to think straight, dangled slackly beneath the eagles, her kicking legs now quite still. She closed her eyes. 'I wish all

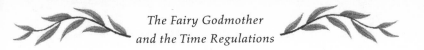

three of you were at the bottom of the sea and that I was a pirate again and none of this had ever happened!'

There was a *whoosh* and a *POP!* and a *BANG!* Five-Fathom Frieda was still in mid-air, held firmly by the Good Manner Eagles, but her fairy godmother suddenly appeared in the rigging of the pirate ship.

'Rule number forty-two,' she said. 'You can't wish the day away. That's meddling with time itself and it's against regulations. Also, it's terribly sad. Don't ever be so bad that you wish your day hadn't happened. This is good advice and it's my last gift to you. If you ever wish the whole day away, you can be pretty sure that it was you, and not the day that should have been different.'

She tossed a scarf over her little shoulder. 'The Wish Committee will hold an investigation into this breach of the space-time regulations – and I no longer have to give you anything that you wish. I have to say I'm not sorry.'

'And so, she loses her own fairy godmother,' Courier remarked quietly from the deck. 'She tested the system, as I thought she would, to complete destruction.'

'You're *my* fairy godmother!' Frieda bellowed. 'You have to do what I say! Whatever I say!'

'Not any more!' Fairy Fata said brightly. 'You came up against time itself. And you will never have a fairy godmother again.'

'Don't want one!' Frieda shouted defiantly as the eagles lowered her slowly to the deck.

There was a little puff of lavender smoke

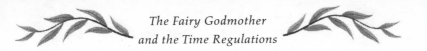
and, with a quick tug on a trailing scarf that had caught in the rigging, the fairy godmother was gone. The tiara disappeared from Frieda's old hat, and the red carpet melted into the mud of the deck, along with the pieces of broken mirror. The pier glass reflected only empty sky.

Bear sighed and started to scrub at the boards of the deck where the red carpet was nothing but a stain. The three Good Manner Eagles released Frieda and stood beside her on the deck, their heads on one side as if they were interested to see what she might do next. She had been so rude that they could not hide their curiosity. In all their years of work on good manners, they had never before met anyone quite so impolite.

Florizella and Bennett came from their

hiding place behind the barrels and nodded a hello at Courier. The Sea Serpent rose silently out of the water and rested its long neck along the bowsprit so it could view them all on deck.

'You're here?' Bennett remarked.

'I take an interest in pirates,' the Sea Serpent explained. It widened it's sapphire eyes at Frieda. 'And, of course, in princesses.'

'Very well done,' Florizella said quietly to Courier.

'I think I saw the main thing at once.'

'You did. Well done,' said Bennett, trying to be gracious about Courier's triumph.

'Was all this drama and trouble for that bear?' the Sea Serpent enquired.

'Yes,' Florizella said.

The Sea Serpent widened its beautiful blue eyes. 'Sssentimental,' it said.

CHAPTER EIGHT

In which everything gets organised so that it can end happily ever after, as it should

Frieda was quite stunned by the arrival of the Good Manner Eagles and the loss of her fairy godmother. 'Do you really have to have such very good manners to be a princess?' she asked Florizella.

'Yes,' Florizella said. 'I've got rid of a lot of the more stupid rules. But we're stuck with the eagles.'

One eagle lifted a feathery eyebrow.

'I mean, we're lucky to still have the eagles,' Florizella said quickly. 'They remind us, whenever we need reminding, of the unending importance of good manners.'

'Key advisors,' Bennett said. 'Highly regarded.'

'Have you come far?' Courier asked one of them.

'I dropped out of the sky like a hurricane,' it replied with quiet pride.

'How d'you ever stand it?' Frieda demanded.

'I suppose different people like different things,' Florizella explained. You probably wouldn't like my things really. You'd definitely prefer your ship to my castle. It's such a nice ship, the good ship *Boney*!'

'What is wrong with you people? Can't you read?' Frieda exclaimed. 'It's *Bonny*! *Bonny*!

After Anne Bonny the pirate.'

'Of course it is,' Courier said smoothly with a little frown at Florizella. 'No wonder you prefer the good ship *Bonny* to a dull old castle.'

'But I was going to have both!' Frieda exclaimed. 'The castle and everything that is yours, as well as keeping my pirate ship. Why shouldn't I have it all?'

The Sea Serpent, itself a rather greedy creature, looked impressed by this ambition.

But Frieda had her eye on Bennett. 'And I was going to have a Prince Charming.' She turned to him. 'Would you marry a pirate?' she asked. 'Me, for instance?'

Bennett looked awkward under her adoring gaze. He opened his mouth to reply, but he could not find the words.

'He wouldn't even marry a princess,' Florizella rescued him. 'He won't even marry me. We're just friends.'

'You'd be much better off being friends with me rather than her,' Frieda told him. 'Why don't you dump her?'

One of the Good Manner Eagles clicked its beak.

Frieda glanced at him. 'Is that rude as well?' she demanded impatiently. 'Really?'

'A bit,' it said.

The Sea Serpent looked down its long nose. 'Fussssssssy,' it said to no one in particular. 'Why don't you tell her about the sssssstake?'

'What stake?' Frieda demanded.

'Where they tie you up,' the Sea Serpent explained. 'And I come to eat you.'

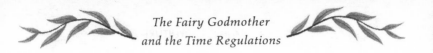
'I'd like to see you try!' she exclaimed.

'Sssssay the word!' the Sea Serpent said eagerly.

'No! No!' Florizella interrupted. 'Sea Serpent! You promised!'

'Would you like to be friends with me?' Frieda asked Bennett coyly.

Bennett bowed in silence.

Frieda turned to Florizella. 'Does he speak? Or is he just ornamental?'

'Yes, of course he speaks!' Florizella said indignantly. 'It's just that a pirate has never proposed marriage to him before. He's surprised. But he's happy to be your friend and so am I.'

'Me too,' agreed Courier.

'You say something,' Frieda ordered Bennett. 'Anything. Now.'

He swallowed. 'Have you come far?'

She looked blankly at him, then she took Florizella by the arm and whispered in her ear. 'I know he's your friend but isn't he a bit weird.'

Florizella, struggling not to laugh, glanced back at Bennett who glared at her. 'Let's all be friends,' she said tactfully. 'Let's all of us be friends.'

'Sssssssertainly,' the Sea Serpent said with an unconvincing smile.

Five-Fathom Frieda looked at them as if she thought it was a trick. 'You mean it?' she asked.

'Yes,' Florizella said. 'If you mean it too?'

Frieda nodded. 'I would like to be friends. I'd like to be friends with you all. Sorry about trying to take Bennett and Courier away from you.' She thought for a moment. 'And the castle. And the pony. And the bear.'

'It's OK,' Florizella said. 'I don't own him. I don't own them. Nobody owns anybody in the Seven Kingdoms. I don't own Bear, or Mammoth, or Sea Serpent, or even Jellybean. And Bear should be free.'

'He can go,' Frieda said carelessly. 'He's a rubbish pirate anyway.'

Bear, silently offended, put down his mop, and went to stand by the gangplank as if he was more than ready to leave.

'I've never had friends before,' Frieda confided. 'I've always made them walk the plank before getting to know them.'

'It does take time, sometimes,' Florizella said fairly.

'But what do you have for lunch?' the Sea Serpent enquired. 'If you have no friends?'

'Burgers,' Frieda answered. 'And grog.'

The Sea Serpent took no further interest in her.

'Well, you have friends now!' Courier assured her. 'Perhaps you would like to visit our castle? Perhaps we could come for a voyage on your ship?'

'You don't think it's too dirty and smelling of old fish?' Frieda asked Bennett, as if his opinion was the only one that mattered.

Of course, it was very dirty and smelly, but Bennett knew that one of the Good Manner Eagles had a yellow eye on him.

'Not at all,' he said.

The eagle nodded approval.

'OK, then,' Frieda said agreeably. 'I'll leave the crew to finish loading, and I'll come and invade your castle at once.'

'Visit,' Courier corrected quietly. 'You mean visit: not invade.'

'Oh yes,' she said, nodding to the eagle. 'A lovely visit and no pillaging.'

Bear ran down the gangplank ahead of them.

'But about Bear . . .' Florizella said. 'There's a bit of a difficulty with him. My father won't have him in the castle. He doesn't want another wild animal.'

'Well, he *is* completely useless,' Frieda said heartlessly. 'I don't blame your dad at all.'

Bear glanced reproachfully at her over his shoulder.

'Don't say that,' Florizella urged her. 'He doesn't speak, but I am sure he understands everything you say.'

'Just like Bennett!' Frieda said cheerfully.

'Bennett speaks,' Florizella corrected her new-found friend. 'But Bear does not. Bennett is a highly educated blue-blood royal, heir to the Land of Deep Lakes, and Bear is a bear, formerly known as the spectacled bear, who doesn't have glasses. He was in a show – it was the Nasty Show.'

'I've been,' Frieda said. 'I didn't pay, and I didn't queue. I just barged in. I liked it a lot.' She turned to Bennett. 'Did you like it? Shall we go again? Like a date?'

Bennett smiled thinly but said nothing.

'We didn't like it,' Florizella said firmly. 'He didn't like it.'

Frieda took her by the arm. 'Look, are you sure he speaks?' she said. 'Because he's hardly

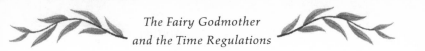

said a word. And, to be honest, it's getting a bit tedious.'

'Sssseldom anything ssssensible,' the Sea Serpent said, swimming alongside the quay.

'He's shy,' Courier told her, trying not to laugh. 'He's very shy around girls.'

Bennett was hugely offended, but still he could not think of anything to say.

'But about Bear . . .' Florizella persisted. They had reached the train station and Mammoth was standing at the rear of the homeward train.

'Hewwo!' he said when he saw his friends. He waved his trunk to the Sea Serpent who was lying half in, half out of the dock, seeing them off. 'Hewwo, Bear!' he said fondly. 'Gwad they found you!'

Bear said nothing, but he looked pleased.

Mammoth's little eyes widened when he saw Five-Fathom Frieda in her big boots and enormous hat. 'Hewwo, Piwate!' he said.

'Hello, me hearty!' Frieda said cheerfully to him. 'You're a fine big elephant!'

'Mammoth,' the Mammoth said.

'You are mammoth,' she agreed.

'No, he *is* a mammoth,' Courier explained. 'From the Ice Age.'

'Gosh, I could use you on one of my ships,' Frieda told him.

'Got to push the twain,' the Mammoth told her, looking alarmed. 'Not weawwy piwate matewial.'

They all got into the train and found seats. Bear stood, holding on to a strap. Mammoth

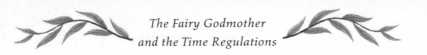

waved an ear in goodbye at the Sea Serpent and started to push the train home.

'I don't know what Daddy King is going to say about us bringing Bear back home,' Florizella whispered to Courier.

'We'll have to do my plan,' Courier told her.

'What was your plan?' Bennett asked quietly.

'R-U-G,' Courier spelled out. 'He has to pretend to be a rug until Daddy King gets used to seeing him around the palace. It'll only be a couple of days.'

'That's all very well,' Bennett said, 'but how do we make him pretend to be a rug?'

'He speaks!' Frieda exclaimed. 'He said a whole sentence!' She was absolutely delighted.

CHAPTER THE LAST

*In which Florizella's father,
the king, demonstrates his
beautiful manners*

*I*t turned out to be easy. Once it was
explained to Bear that he had to lie
completely flat on the floor and do nothing
else whenever the king was in the castle, he
was quite agreeable. In the last week, he had
been a not-very-popular attraction in the
Nasty Show, a wild bear, a fairy-godmother
wish and a pirate deckhand. He was quite
prepared to be a rug for a change. He thought

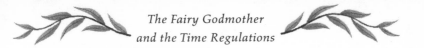
he would enjoy the rest.

'But don't snore!' Bennett exclaimed as Bear lay down, closed his eyes and drifted off to sleep. 'You'll completely ruin the illusion if you snore. When you snore, you look like a lazy bear fast asleep before the fire. Not like a rug at all.'

Bear opened his eyes and bared his teeth.

'Better,' Bennett approved. 'Much better. Can you keep your eyes open when the king walks past and not blink?'

Bear tried a glassy stare.

'Really excellent,' said Courier.

'And we'll feed you,' Florizella assured him. 'We'll bring you regular meals whenever Daddy King goes out.'

'He goes out often,' Courier promised him. 'Kingly work.'

'Kingly work!' Five-Fathom Frieda scoffed, poking Bear with her toe. 'You can't really call it work.'

'What you do isn't really work, either,' Courier pointed out.

Frieda drew her enormous cutlass. 'Say that again and I'll behead you!' she shouted. She shot a quick glance out of the hall window but the circling Good Manner Eagle was high above the battlements. It had no interest in Frieda's bad manners now she was not royal.

'Now just stop,' said Florizella, leading the way up the stairs to the gallery that ran all around the hall. 'Frieda, put your cutlass away. This is what it's like to have a friend. You don't always agree with them, but you stay friends all the same. You might even have a quarrel,

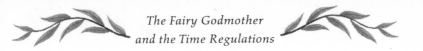

but you make it up. You don't behead your friends to end an argument.'

Frieda glanced at Bennett. 'Is that right?'

Bennett was awkward. 'It is right,' he said. 'But you don't need a boy to tell you so. Girls know as much as boys do.'

'Girls are as good as boys?' Frieda was amazed by this simple truth.

'Quite as good,' Bennett said.

'So a girl doesn't have to shout and wear big boots if she wants to be heard?'

'A girl should be heard just as much as a boy,' Florizella told her. 'Whatever she or he chooses to wear. And you can be friends with someone without shouting at them or beheading them. And you can check things out with me or Bennett.'

'Or even Courier,' Bennett offered. 'He knows things too – quite surprising things.'

Frieda looked absolutely baffled. 'This is a lot more complicated than being the Terror of the Seas,' she said.

They walked along the gallery past suits of armour and smiling portraits of the royal family. Frieda only looked at the pictures with heaps of treasure or ships.

'Anyone can be mean,' Courier pointed out. 'Anyone can be a bully. Anyone can go around beheading people if they've got a cutlass. But it takes a clever person to be kind, and a particularly clever person to have a cutlass and not to behead people.'

'I am that,' Frieda said, shoving her cutlass back in its scabbard. 'I'm a clever person. I

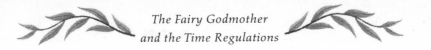

am a particularly clever person.'

'*Phew*,' said Florizella to herself, rather feeling that they had got a long way with Five-Fathom Frieda rather quickly. She led the way down the stairs from the gallery to the great hall.

'And attractive,' Frieda said with a little glance at Bennett. 'Clever and attractive. Don't you think so, Bennett?'

Bennett opened and closed his mouth, and found he had absolutely nothing to say.

'Look, he's gone off again,' Frieda said irritably to Florizella. 'He's as talkative as your rug.'

'Bear,' Florizella said.

'Same thing,' Frieda said crossly. She turned to Bennett. 'Say something!' she ordered. 'Anything.'

Bennett flushed with embarrassment.

'Anything!' she repeated. 'Tell me something I don't know.'

'You spell Bonny with two *n*'s and no *e*!' Bennett, cornered suddenly, burst into speech.

Frieda was amazed. 'You do?'

Bennett nodded.

'Don't start that again,' she told him. 'Carry on speaking. But how do you know that?'

'School. I learned how to spell in school.'

'Never been,' she said. 'Never needed it.'

'Except when you painted the name of your ship on the prow?' Courier suggested.

'*Bonny*?'

'Two *n*'s,' Florizella confirmed.

'Well, you've taught me something,' Frieda admitted. 'Quite a lot of things actually. And, in return, I'll teach you how to be a pirate. Will you come for a raid?'

'A sail?' Florizella suggested.

'Oh, as you like.'

'We will!' said Florizella as they arrived in the great hall where a huge fire was burning in the grate and a handsome bearskin rug was laid on the floor.

The king was standing in front of the fire, getting warm. He turned when they came in. 'Don't step on the rug,' he warned them. 'It sort of squeaks if you do. It's new, not quite settled in yet.'

'Probably needs a drop of oil,' Florizella said reassuringly.

'It's a great rug,' Bennett remarked. 'It looks very good there, in front of the fire.'

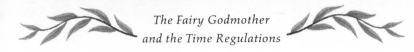

'It does, doesn't it?' The king was pleased with his bearskin rug. Bear lay very still, with wide-open eyes and a big smile that showed his teeth. 'You know, I've always wanted a rug in front of this fireplace. And now – look – it's just turned up.'

'Like you wished for it,' Courier suggested.

'Undootedly! *Undootedly!* Like a fairy godmother granted my wish,' the king agreed, laughing at his own joke. He caught sight of Five-Fathom Frieda. 'Oh, hello,' he said vaguely. 'Miss . . . Ms . . .'

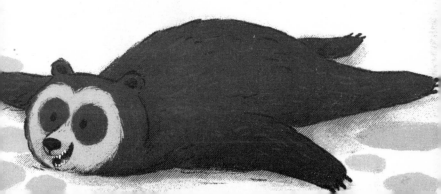

'Captain,' Florizella told him. 'This is Captain Five-Fathom Frieda of the pirate ship *Bonny*. (Two *n*'s.) Just visiting, not invading. Just friendly, not beheading anyone. Not even Courier.'

'Good, good,' said the king. 'Jolly good show. Have you come far?'

The End